The characters in "Whatever Ye Sow" are fictitious.

ISBN:978-1-926633-51-0

Printed by The McMaster Innovation Press

Whatever Ye ? Sow

By

Patricia Kortland

Dedication

This book is dedicated to the descendants of Scottish immigrants to Canada and the curious: those who want to understand the cultural climate of the 1850's – Niagara Falls to Montreal.

Contents

Foreword

My interest in history was ignited when I was very young, perhaps four or five. My Grandpa Robertson shared remembrances while he puffed on his pipe and I sat at his knee. He had responded to the call "*Go West Young Man, Go West*" early in 1900. He built a sod shack on his acreage. When he awoke one morning, he saw that a blizzard had blown snow under his door and right across the buffalo robe that covered him. His first crop of wheat looked good and nearly ready to harvest. He drove Black Barney into Estevan for groceries. On his return he found his crop gone and his shack destroyed by a wild prairie fire. Kind town folk took him in and he turned his hand to accounting, then banking. One night, he and a friend foiled a robbery attempt by shining a large kerosene spotlight on the getaway car of the Dillinger Gang.

Over the many years I have visited locations that take you back in time. Several historical homes in Toronto were fascinating. Strolling on the parade grounds at Fort York, Fort George and Fort Henry I could visualize a day in the lives of their residents. Visits to Black Creek Pioneer Village, Upper Canada Village and Ameliasburgh Museum were exhilarating. And fortunately for me the old villages of Picton, Niagara-on-the-Lake, Dundas, Oakville, and Merrickville have preserved many of their early buildings' facades. But these visits provided small pieces to a larger puzzle.

I sought a fuller picture of the region and its activities in the 1850's around the north shore of Lake Ontario and the banks (on the Canadian side) of the Niagara and St. Lawrence Rivers. And so my research began and the story unfolded with the aid of my Scottish heroine, Christine.

Some of my discoveries were amazing! Who would have imagined a hotel in Niagara Falls that could accommodate three to four hundred people? I had no idea that the populations of Toronto (25,000) and Montreal (60,000) were as large. Roads were spreading quickly and were being macadamized. Farmlands were being cleared. Lake Ontario and its major rivers were still dominated by boats of various types. Railroad construction was in its infancy. Many settlers continued to create rich lives socially and culturally – wanting to forget the adversity that they had left behind. Competent organizers and visionaries, mainly from Britain, came to establish departments of government, education, justice, medicine, and religion. We have all been blessed by this fact.

I wish to thank friends who have encouraged me to complete this work. Research assistance was provided by staff at the Meaford Public Library and by my husband Ben who used his computer and photocopier. Members of the Harvest Writers Guild patiently heard a chapter a month for a year and half. And I am most grateful to Don and Nancy Hamilton for their excellent work typing and editing this manuscript. The reviewers, Elizabeth Scarlett and Garry McEachern, receive my plaudits.

Chapter 1
Scotland 1854

The year 1792 was called *"The Year of the Sheep"* in Scotland. It was so named because Sir John Sinclair of Ulbster introduced a large number of Cheviot sheep to his lands. He wanted small tenant farmers to combine property and capital, to hire herdsmen in common and purchase a small flock of three hundred sheep.

Many landowners and highland lairds had other ideas. Often living a high life they were bothered by creditors. And graziers of the lowlands hungered for land acquisitions and the highest profits attainable. Sheep, providing wool and mutton, were a more lucrative choice than cattle.

And thus began a period of over fifty years called *"The Clearances"*. A chief or laird, often absent, would assign the factor or tacksman to order all his tenants off the land. These devastated folk had to remove their livestock and furniture and could, in some cases, remove the wood from their shanties before they were demolished or set on fire. Often their crops and gardens had to be abandoned. One group from Lord Stafford's northern holdings was offered small plots of land on the rocky west coast of Scotland where cattle couldn't graze or food grown. He expected them all to fish or sign aboard an immigrant ship for America or Australia. Often factors and lairds required help from local sheriffs and their officers or even demanded the army to drive these unfortunate people out.

It was an unhappy land, devoid of people content and satisfied with their lot. Starvation threatened and was a reality. Families were split up. So many had left and were still leaving for new lands. They were prepared to work hard to re-establish themselves. Sometimes in order to obtain a passage fee they would be indentured to a wealthy settler. If after a month or longer at sea, frequently in steerage and in dire conditions they arrived healthy, they were most fortunate.

And thus it was that Christine MacDonald found herself with all her meagre possessions on the dock at Greenock out of Glasgow, awaiting the loading of the ship, *"Good Intent"*, bound for Quebec City, Lower Canada. The year was 1854. She was being sent to be chatelaine at her Uncle Randolph's country estate near Oakdale, Upper Canada. He was her Father's older brother and an established lawyer. Her Father, a minister of the Church of Scotland was grateful that her passage providing a small cabin had been prepaid.

After disembarking at Quebec, she boarded a smaller steamboat, the *"Champion"* and traveled the St. Lawrence River to Montreal. Following a brief rest in the city, she journeyed beyond to Toronto, recently York, located on the north shore of Lake Ontario. From there she traveled by stagecoach to her final destination.

Chapter 2
Toronto to Oakdale

Lightning flashed, mud-laden wheels rolled clumsily on, heavy hooves thumped and splashed as the burdened, giant spectre of a stagecoach lurched in spasms toward its destination. *"After two days of heavy rain the condition of the Lake Road was deplorable"*, noted Christine's diary.

The Toronto to Niagara coach was late. Christine peered through the isinglass. Dark box-shaped houses, then the occasional store appeared in lines, orderly compared to the jagged ruts revealed by the intermittent flashes of lightning. The vehicle jerked suddenly right, passengers groping for something solid to hold.

The only welcoming haven offered the jostled passengers thus far was Birch Hill Inn – porch and window lanterns flaming in the tyrannical night. Spring rains had often kept the kitchen staff late. A broth, dark-thick with succulent secrets chortled on the salon hob. In the cook's domain the giant kettle jumped with hot water for tea and the warming oven guarded its recently baked scones.

The horses too sensed a haven here. They strained against their dripping harnesses, then came to a rearing halt with "*Whoa there! Easy now!*" at the glistening porch. The inn bell was jangled; a customary signal – two long, then two short.

Inside folks paced and stretched to loosen up their joints. They clustered in small groups to thaw hands and feet at the large roaring fire. There was a middle-aged couple returning to Milltown; they were Samuel Jameson, a weaver and his wife, Elizabeth. Young John Just, apprentice to a cabinetmaker was dropping off to sleep in a fireside chair. He was returning home to Niagara to continue to recuperate from consumption. Two gentlemen tailors, Joshua Van Allen and Jed Colburne, had just completed their apprenticeships. Joshua had obtained work in the immediate area, while Jed would move on to Dundas to try his luck. They both were suitably turned out in vests and frock coats – good samples indeed they bore.

Meanwhile the innkeeper and stable boy, dark mounds in their dripping oilskins, assisted the coachmen to dislodge carpetbags and trunks which emerged from beneath a drenched tarpaulin.

Mrs. Chisholm, candlestick in hand, requested signatures for the register. Then following their late meal she led the ladies upstairs to their rooms. Christine's looked over the main street. The Jamesons were settled across the hall. The lad, John, already heavily asleep was loaded on to a bench near the fire and covered with a quilt. The two young tailors were guided by candlelight to a shared accommodation at the rear of the building.

Christine moved her candles to the corner of her room. Shielding her eyes from their light she peered and strained to see through the wet glass. She wondered, "*What is my new town like? Are people congenial here? Will I be happy with Uncle Randolph?*" Lightning flashed again allowing box-like gabled images to show briefly, then disappear. She flung her hooded cloak to the bed, unfastened her bag and found her nightgown and socks. Gazelle-like she jumped up into the gown and down into the woolen socks with almost one move. A bed warmer had been placed beneath her covers, but it had been removed to another bed. She smiled as she remembered her Father giving his parting gift – a pair of socks meant for him. "*But Father, ye'll have to wait a month for another pair!*" she reminded him. "*Don't ye worry"* he said, *"our Margaret mends well."* He had heard that Canada was bitter cold in winter. Well, this was early May and yet the air was damp and penetrating.

The tailors were talked out and extinguished their candles. The coachmen shared quarters with the stable boy. The pattering of feet in the upper hall ceased and a deep peace overtook the place.

Only the stable boy was awake to greet the breakfast gong next morning. The others in residence arose quickly when they recognized the tantalizing aroma of muffins and bacon. The refreshed group filed downstairs and took places at the long pine table, suggested by the innkeeper's wife. Mrs. Chisholm was the light of the morning – smiling and greeting each one most pleasantly.

Christine was placed between the youth and the married woman as propriety required. She responded to many queries briefly although her brain raced ahead. *"What a bore these trivialities,"* crossed her mind. She almost jumped up from the table at the sharpness of her thoughts. *"Hmm, I'd much rather be between those good-looking tailors, taking in some of their experiences,"* she mused as she continued to sip her tea. The sudden mischievous sparkle of her blue eyes did not go unnoticed. Joshua, the young tailor was quietly amused.

Chapter 3
Settling In At Bon Adventure

Christine's diary soon recorded her first meeting with Uncle Randolph.

"He arrived at the inn early morning, in a neat chaise driven by a servant. He is taller than Father, but similar in that he has thick graying hair, moustache and deep blue eyes. He bowed over my hand and his eyes twinkled as I made my curtsey. His man placed my bag at the base of the vehicle and then assisted me to my seat beside Uncle. As the morgan trotted toward the estate my uncle asked many questions: "*How is yer Father's health, and Edith's?*" I was pleased to assure him they were fine. He then continued to inquire about many of our Scottish friends."

The long driveway, lined by vibrant young maples ended in a circle centred by a fountain. The fifteen-room brick edifice fronted by double white doors and pillars was most impressive. The coach house sat on the left half way up the drive. Her uncle lifted her down and led her to the front step. His staff, a housekeeper-cook, parlor maid, butler and house boy stood in a line to greet her. They made their bows and curtseys to "Miss

Christine" then dispersed to carry out duties necessitated by her arrival.

The butler carried in her carpetbag and the housekeeper instructed the maid to take Christine directly upstairs. Up the circular stairs they climbed to the second floor hall. Her bedroom was on the lake side of the house. She insisted that she would unpack her few belongings herself. The maid was dismissed. Christine rushed to the window to take in the mid-morning view of the lake. Its waters glistened and rippled. A single masted skiff skimmed along in the steady breeze. A two-masted schooner made its way across the horizon. It was likely traveling from Niagara to Toronto bearing passengers and cargo.

She was scheduled to join her Uncle for lunch at midday. This was her second encounter and she expected it to be as pleasant as the first. After a cold repast, Christine was led to the parlor. Randolph placed her opposite him in a lady's chair near the fireplace.

"Yer friend, Edith asked me to bring ye this", she added. And she presented him with a small box.

"Oh my! Oh my!" was all he could say as he fought back tears – holding a small gold

locket aloft. Later she learned that he had received a likeness of Edith and a lock of her fair hair – as a token of lost love.

"My dear Christine," he said *"ye do so remind me of Edith when she was yer age. I'm so pleased to receive this gift!"* Edith had married a Glasgow businessman. She had wished to remain in Scotland and had turned down Randolph's proposal of marriage and the opportunity of emigration. Thus he had lost his first true love. But she had certainly not forgotten him. A flicker of remorse crossed his face. He stood and turned to place his treasure in a nearby drawer.

As he recovered he said, *"Shall we do a wee bit of sight-seeing this afternoon or would ye still be fatigued after yer long journey?"*

No nineteen year old of good constitution could object to a new adventure so she replied, *"Aach, I'm quite fine, Uncle Randolph. I'd most certainly like to see the toon!"*

As they traveled by chaise westward to Oakdale they passed several farms. Men and women were busy plowing or clearing the land with oxen or heavy draft horses. It was planting time. Many tree stumps and brush piles were being burned – and smoke curled skyward here and there. The smell of the land and smoke mingled in her nostrils. Her Uncle, at the reins, directed her attention to several buildings on the north side of the lake road.

"There's O'Reilly's Tavern where many's an altercation has taken place," he informed her. The one next was the bakery with a large front window offering rye bread, buns and pastries. The doctor's house came next, his horse and buggy in the lane; he was quite ready to head out on a call. Their Kirk, the Church of Scotland followed. It was constructed of grey-stone – simply but beautifully fashioned by Scottish masons, recent immigrants. They trotted past family homes where owners were busy planting their vegetable gardens. A shoemaker's shop came next and beside it, the tailor's. The door flew open and Joshua Van Allen hurried out carrying a man's suit – on his way to deliver it. They slowed the morgan.

"Hello Mr. Van Allen," Christine called. *"This is my Uncle Randolph MacDonald."* Joshua tipped his hat. *"I know yer master, McKlintock,"* her uncle informed him.

Christine asked to alight at the General Store so that she could buy thread for Mrs. McKay. Their housekeeper had promised to help Christine make a day dress from a soft green chambray, the material a gift from her Uncle. Randolph drove on to the blacksmith's to have the morgan's shoes checked. He decided that the completion of the grand tour would have to take place at another time.

Chapter 4
The Chatelaine

The next afternoon Christine was summoned to her Uncle's office. As she sat erectly in a leather chair, she poised her pencil to note his requirements in her journal. She was to carry several keys on her belt: one for the wine-cellar, another for the silver chest, another for the pantry, one for her bedroom and another for an attic chest containing family treasures. Thus she would be on call mostly to Mrs. McKay, the housekeeper.

Christine was expected to plan the meals with her and give more direction to the housemaid. She could also hire extra help for large dinner parties – or extensive house-cleanings in spring or fall. As Christine loved flowers, she requested her uncle's permission to help plant them, harvest them and arrange them in the grand house. She was to help him to catch up correspondence at rushed times. She was to be at his side as hostess to great dignitaries and friends on visits or if they attended special house dinners. Also, she was to be his partner when he was invited out. He would require tea in his office at precisely 3 o'clock. Supper was to be served at 6:30 sharp.

Since her Mother's death, her Father had been very satisfied with her running of their modest home. She was quick to learn, of pleasant personality and hard working. Christine recalled his compliments – then wondered if she was really capable of handling all this! Little did she know that she would soon be tested.

A week after receiving her list of duties, Robert, the butler, asked her to join her uncle in his office. His dark oak desktop was strewn with papers and he spoke hastily, "*There's a new bank being established in toon, lassie. We'll hold a celebratory dinner for the owner, McIsaac and his wife. Here's the guest list. We'll hold it Saturday eve mid-June. Ye have three weeks to prepare. Off ye go!*"

Christine closed the door swiftly, but paused for a moment to assess the situation. She counted twenty-four people: most would attend in couples: two general store owners, Kirk minister, doctor, boat builder, tannery owner, lumber and wheat storage owner, manager of the custom's house, post master, bank manager, bakery owner, and clerks of the bank and custom's house. Counting Uncle and herself, twenty-six would have to be seated.

"Don't panic now!" she chided herself aloud. *"Mrs. McKay, Mrs. McKay, we're to plan a dinner!"* she rushed into the kitchen through the swinging door. *"We'll talk in half an hour, lassie after I finish these wee pasties,"* the cook remarked.

Christine paced the early spring garden. She went there to think and to break through some of the tension she felt. As they met at the kitchen table they divided responsibilities. Mrs. McKay would see that the suckling pig and eggs for the lemon sponge dessert were ordered immediately from neighbouring farmers. The houseboy would bring carrots, turnips and potatoes from the root cellar. He would buy fresh salmon from the Indians who fished the lake. Their occasional gardener who had a green house on site would provide early broad beans for their table. Crabapple preserves, extra candles and wine could be purchased at their favourite general store. Christine would do this soon. To have the invitations printed, she would visit the local newspaper office as soon as possible.

On Sunday morning at Kirk she approached her new friend, Laura Ross: *"Would ye know of a couple who could serve well for three days? Uncle Randolph has planned a dinner for mid-June and we'll need extra help!"*

"Well now, I know Joan and John McRae. I'll make contact for ye!" she offered gladly.

At her Uncle's insistence, Christine agreed to have an evening gown made for the occasion. She chose a deep blue silk, an off the shoulder creation touched with white lace. Its full glistening skirt over crinolines swished as she walked. She felt quite regal.

The grand evening arrived. The long oak table in the dining room had been carefully set and glistened with silver and white linen in the candlelight. Her late tulips made a beautiful centerpiece. The clip-clop of horses' hooves was heard on the drive and soon many couples had presented their invitations to the butler. In the reception hall, Christine and her Uncle greeted them warmly. Screens which divided the music room from the parlor were removed to make this front room even larger. Lacking a piper, the houseboy in his best, led them to the dining-room playing a Scottish march on his flute.

Randolph MacDonald made a speech of introduction and toasted the new banker, McIsaac and his wife. They were pleased indeed with this special reception. The success of the occasion was the talk of the town for several weeks.

Chapter 5
Unexpected Events

July came and went. Christine was kept busy with the flower garden and with entertaining small groups of over-night guests. Her uncle's property lay along a half-mile of lakefront and from time to time Christine would walk along the shore accompanied by her uncle's Gordon setters.

One afternoon in early August, Christine and the dogs were exploring a westward section of the shoreline, when she stopped for a moment to view the lake's transports. A small steam-boat was progressing eastward and numerous canoes were a safe distance from shore, their native rowers fishing for salmon or lake trout. At first softly, then more clearly came the Scottish air "*Annie Laurie*" sung sweetly by a highland lass. Christine called the dogs to her side – and most curious – tiptoed toward the sound. As she rounded a bushy hillock she came upon a sod shack that was partly dug out of a high embankment. Smoke curled lazily from an outdoor cooking pit. She now realized that the song was sung as a lullaby for a fretting bairn. She was surprised to find Joan McRae seated on an ancient rocking chair in the shack's open door, cradling her child. Her singing stopped short and she said in surprise, *"Miss Christine, what brings ye here?"*

"I've just come down to see the loch, Mrs. McRae. Where is your good man at this time o' the day?"

"He's had a wee bit of luck. He's helping clear land for a new farmer up Trafalgar Road."

"How is it ye are settled on Uncle's land?" Christine queried.

"John and I were indentured to old farm folk near toon. While on our crossing they took the small pox and both passed awa'. We were left with nay home ner work. Yer friend, Mrs. Ross has been good. Yer uncle's housekeeper gave us the right to be here and slips us vitals, sometimes," offered Joan.

"Thank ye for your help at our dinner. I'll try to visit again soon," Christine promised on parting. *"How on the earth could they survive the winter in such a hovel?"* she mused.

Back at the estate, Christine began to plan to assist the couple and their child. She had been deeply affected by the unexpected meeting. She would speak privately to the minister of the Kirk. She would boldly approach anyone who had a building to spare. And so Christine arranged the loan of a simple, dry shed for the McRaes until their circumstance had improved. After their relocation, Christine often brought them fresh produce or baking. She was gratified to see the child healthy and happy.

Earlier that same month her Uncle Randolph had traveled by stagecoach to Toronto. He had visited a fellow advocate, Mr. Cockburn for a week. A few days after his return he came down with a high fever, chills and vomiting. Dr. Black was called in for a diagnosis and treatment. Christine learned that it was malaria that he had contracted. The numerous swamps edging Lake Ontario were breeding places for the nasty mosquito that carried the malady.

Randolph was seriously ill and Christine did her utmost to care for him. She bathed his forehead when the fever peaked and sang many of his favorite Scottish ballads to hasten sleep. She requested a chicken and vegetable broth from the kitchen. With his butler's help they propped him up in bed and spooned it into his mouth – happy when most of it trickled down his throat. Robert changed his nightshirt when it became drenched with sweat. Two weeks dragged by – then the fever broke and a deep and restful sleep followed. His appetite gradually returned in the third week. At last he was able to be on his feet. For a few days he needed her arm for support.

"Lassie, I'm so grateful to ye for pulling me through," her Uncle repeated time and time again. He was convinced that she had helped save his life.

"Aaach, Uncle, I'm so happy I was here to help," she'd return.

Through the summer months she attended Kirk faithfully. The young widow, Laura Ross had become a close friend. They took tea together mid-week and quilted with a group caring for the poor of the young settlement. Joshua Van Allen also attended Kirk weekly. He made a point of seeking her out to ask of her welfare. To end his conversation he said, *"I'm receiving a small monthly raise. I'm also starting an account at the new bank."* As he came to the end of the sentence, his eyes twinkled and his mouth formed a suggestive smile. But Christine was much too busy with harvesting and preserving at the estate and settling in the McRaes to notice any innuendo.

After a rigorous day in early September, Christine excused herself from her uncle's company to go to bed early. She lit the small oil lamp, made a short diary entry, said her prayers and drifted off. She was overtired and tossed and turned.

"I awoke – I heard a groaning sound down the hall. Someone was in pain. The clock chimed eleven. The sound stopped but I still lay stiff in fright. Next morning I asked Mrs. McKay if she had heard anything. Her answer, "No." But of course, her bedroom off the kitchen was too far from the source. Uncle had breakfasted before me and was still catching up on work after his illness. That afternoon he had a business engagement in town. I decided to investigate the source of the sound. My bedroom key had unlocked other rooms on the second floor. I checked Uncle's room as well as the guest and storage rooms. I turned the key in the lock of the last room. The door squeaked open jerkily. The room was dark and cheerless. Much to my shock I saw instruments of bondage strewn around: a chair, stocks, handcuffs, whip – I closed it swiftly. I had seen the housekeeper's son, Stuart come from that room. I dared to imagine what was going on there! I was afraid for my life! I was

going to Laura's for tea and would share my awful secret!"

After hearing Christine's incredible revelation, Laura offered her sanctuary. The very next morning Christine confronted her Uncle Randolph.

In a voice shaking with emotion she began: "*What is this I've found in the end room – a torture chamber? I am packed to stay with Mrs. Ross. I'll not return 'til I've heard better of ye! What of that poor boy Stuart?"* she demanded angrily.

Her uncle was caught off guard. "*Ah, lassie calm down! It's not the boy that's hurt – but myself! Don't go!"* She turned swiftly about – strode out of the dining room – chin held high. The trap had arrived at the door. Christine helped to load her small trunk and carpetbag. Eyes flashing in anger – she climbed quickly aboard. The driver recognized her haste and with a click of his tongue and a snap of the reins, they were off.

Chapter 6
A Chance Meeting

Christine and Laura continued their routine of teatimes and quilting. Christine did not attend Kirk, though, so as not to meet her Uncle, but accompanied Laura to the Church of England, St. George's.

Early the second week, Laura received a letter stating that a new acquaintance, Duchess Janine La Fleur was arriving at week's end from Montreal.

Laura shared what she knew about her. *"We met last summer at a ball held by the lieutenant-governor of Lower Canada in Montreal. My husband, Lawrence was alive then. She came from England to visit her married sister, Louise. She told me that her grandparents had left France in 1783 just two years before the Revolution. They brought a title and much money with them – enough to establish a tannery. Then Janine's parents expanded the business to include the manufacture of gloves, boots and shoes. An English army contract brought them considerable wealth during the Napoleonic Wars. Not married, Janine spends much time traveling, quite enjoying herself!"*

Christine recalled Scotland's connection with France during the reign of Mary Queen of Scots and her son, James VI. The University of Edinburgh where her Father had studied provided classes in French. Her Father prided himself on speaking it fluently – and thus provided several years of study for Christine and her brother. Christine had managed the language quite well during her short stays in Quebec and Montreal. She would certainly like to maintain her fluency and was looking forward to Duchess Janine La Fleur's arrival.

Late Friday afternoon the stage from Toronto arrived at the Birch Hill Inn. The duchess was so happy to touch her feet on solid ground. Laura hired a young fellow with a cart to bear the duchess's luggage to her home, just a few minutes walk from the inn. The ladies were surprised that she traveled without a servant or companion.

"Mes chers, servants are most difficult to find here. Ma fille died of the small pox in Quebec and now I am quite alone!" she answered. She explained that she was invited to the wedding of Christabetta, daughter of Sir Howard McNair, governor general of the Canadas. The service would be held a week to-morrow at the

Father's estate in Hamilton. As a wedding gift she had bought a linen tablecloth and napkins, exquisitely embroidered by the sisters of a Montreal convent. The two young women were very impressed.

That evening they questioned her eagerly about events in the cultural life of Quebec and Montreal. "*Who of importance have you met? What concerts did you attend? Did you see a play by Molière?*"

The McNair wedding was just a week off. Christine and Laura wanted to make the Duchess's visit interesting. Wherever they went Mademoiselle La Fleur strode out ahead of them, tapping her umbrella as she waited for them to scurry to her side. Her ramrod bearing frightened some, but the girls were so busy trying to keep up they paid no mind. They took her up river by canoe, paddled by a local trapper-guide. They visited the docks to watch the loading of wheat and oak for England. They visited a gristmill on the river. Janine also ordered a grand hat at the tailor's for the wedding. There they were warmly greeted by Joshua.

The time approached for the duchess's departure. She lamented daily of not having a servant who would be her traveling companion. Christine decided that she could no longer burden Laura, so she boldly offered her services. Surprised but grateful Janine settled – three pounds a month on her. Her travel, food and accommodation would be provided gratis. Laura was charged with reporting to her on her Uncle Randolph. Her housekeeper was Mrs. McKay's cousin – so she would have an inside ear.

Christine arranged two passages to Hamilton with a schooner captain. She was excited about seeing a new location. The wedding would be a special event as well, but she would not know for a while if she would be invited to attend.

Christine packed most of her items the morning before departure. Then she assisted Mademoiselle La Fleur to pack three trunks. What lovely gowns she touched! *"I'll have my own blue silk for special occasions,"* she thought.

A trap came for the ladies. Laura hugged Christine at the garden gate. *"Ye ken I'll miss ye. I'll not forget to write ye. I have two addresses."* Duchess La Fleur exclaimed, *"Merci and prenez guarde"* which meant thank you and take care. As they set off, she saluted. Christine daubed tears from her eyes, but struggled to control herself as she met the Duchess's stern gaze.

The dock was bustling with activity. Stevedores were shouting, cargo was being moved out of a ship's hold and their luggage was being whisked away. The first mate of the *"Sea Gull"* assisted the ladies aboard. They were told that the trip would take about two hours, wind favorable. They would dock below the McNair estate and would require transport to it.

The schooner glided out of Oakdale Harbor. Christine's fine golden hair was blown by the wind. Her blue eyes sparkled and her cheeks were rosy. She looked lovely and many a man's eyes turned her way. The Duchess noticed. But Christine was studying the shore – counting the new residences there. She also recognized many water birds, identifying them for the Duchess.

Chapter 7
At Pentland Castle

On their arrival at Hamilton's MacKay's Wharf, the first mate summoned a rental carriage and helped them alight. He ordered two of his shipmen to load their luggage.

In about twenty minutes they arrived at the gatehouse of the estate. The keeper directed their driver to take them to the front entrance. Christine rang the bell. They introduced themselves to the butler and he ushered them into the front hall. He then directed the driver to deliver their trunks and bags to the guesthouse located on the east corner of the grounds.

"Mr. McNair is in court today. However, Miss Christabetta is at home and I will have it announced that you have arrived," said the man, bowing politely. A maid was dispatched to notify her mistress while the two ladies were led to the parlor and shown seats. Without a word they both admired the furnishings and marveled at the size of the place. They had not seen such a residence in either of the Canadas.

"Miss Christabetta," announced the maid. A lovely girl about Christine's age swept into

the room and made a quick curtsey before the Duchess.

"How nice to see you again Duchess! How kind of you to attend my wedding to-morrow! Please introduce me to your companion," requested the bride-to-be. After satisfying her curiosity, Christabetta ordered tea and sandwiches. *"You are to stay a week, surely. Father will want you to see the town. While you're here, please enjoy the fall gardens,"* she invited.

The duchess declared that she wished a rest and insisted that they could walk to their residence. Parasols up, the two ladies headed up a path east of the main building. Within a few minutes they had arrived at the dark oak door of the guesthouse, had rung the bell and had been greeted by the housekeeper. They were led up the carpeted stairs to the second floor and presented separate rooms. The duchess asked Christine to wake her not later than five o'clock so that she might dress for the half past six supper.

Christine got settled in – unpacked her clothes and toiletries. She drew on her tartan cloak and decided to explore the grounds. She followed a second path that led toward the stables. Beyond, a sweet-smelling apple orchard beckoned. Two pickers were filling a bushel basket for the kitchen. They offered her two rosy ones to enjoy. She put them into her deep pocket and thanked them kindly.

As she crossed the knoll on the lake side of the great house, a pleasant male voice sang, "*Did you ever see a lassie, a lassie, a lassie, did you ever see a lassie go this way and that?*"

"*Impudent,*" she thought. But when the handsome young man in uniform caught up with her she was quite charmed. He bowed over her gloved hand and confidently said "*I'm Lieutenant Charles Conners of General McNair's local militia. I'm here for the wedding, are you?*" Christine answered in the affirmative and they continued to chat about their countries of birth, the expanding economy of the Canadas and the Rebellion of 1837 and how it had influenced the governance of the new union.

Christine asked for the time. He consulted his pocket watch; it was thirty minutes past four. She excused herself and quickly headed back to the guesthouse to rouse the Duchess and to help her dress for supper.

Janine La Fleur was awake and waiting for Christine to unpack her trunks. "*What supper gown will we wear, ma chère?"* she asked. Christine was shaking out a rust taffeta adorned with cream-colored lace and said, *"Aye, this will be perfect!"* As the Duchess's traveling companion she was to be at Sir Howard McNair's table, too. So she rushed to don a simple velvet burgundy dress that she had sown herself. To be even more elegant she placed a large Belgian lace collar around her shoulders and tied it once at the front. She smiled with satisfaction as she consulted her mirror.

As they arrived at the great doors beneath the portico, the door opened and Mr. McNair himself, was there to greet them. He conducted them to the parlor to await the butler's announcement that dinner would be served. Christine was escorted to her place at the glistening dinner table by Lieutenant Conners.

Sir Howard McNair's parents had been United Empire Loyalists – and discussion arose from this fact. *"Where have most of the immigrants settled?"* asked Christine of McNair.

"Around the edges of our major lakes," initially he responded. *"But now they've pushed*

well inland looking for good farm land or a water source for a mill."

"How have they managed to survive?" questioned Conners who had recently arrived from England.

"At first Simcoe granted 200 acres of land to early settlers, mostly German and Dutch coming from United States. They had to build a home, clear five acres and lay down a quarter mile of road in front of their house. After Simcoe left in 1796 tracts of land were purchased from the natives. Smaller pieces were reserved for the clergy of the Church of England. Others were sold publicly by the Canada Company. After our war with The United States, many people loyal to Britain received land grants when they moved here," he reported.

"We have heard of your role in the Rebellion of 1837," added the Duchess. *"You were in charge of one thousand men at Toronto, we understand and you helped regain the peace."*

Sir McNair cleared his throat and nodded in the affirmative – but changed the subject. He wanted them to know that he had founded a new bank and that he was most interested in railways that would assist in a developing country.

The men retired to the governor's large office where they continued their discussion and smoked. The ladies unanimously agreed to walk the circumference of the building and asked a maid for their wraps. Christine and the duchess bade the group good night when they reached the path to the guesthouse.

The wedding day arrived. It was sunny and comfortably warm. Household staff rushed about on last minute errands. Baskets in hand, two maids were selecting fresh vegetables from the eastern garden and another two picking fresh fall flowers. In the stable yard, the grooms were exercising several horses. The team would take the newlyweds on their honeymoon.

The ladies took a light lunch at their residence. The wedding service was set for two that afternoon. Appropriately gowned in their silks with lace, reticules prepared with handkerchiefs, combs and smelling salts, Christine and Duchess Janine La Fleur raised their parasols and strolled to the portico of the main residence.

A fine carriage arrived as they entered, a family of five chatting excitedly. The two ladies were greeted by the butler who then handed them over to two ushers and they were led to seats arranged in the parlor. A lecturn had been placed at the centre of the three long bay windows. The sun cast interesting shadows on the walls. Soft music was playing near the fireplace on the left. Then the pianist and violinist began a march and all eyes turned toward the French doors. Sir Howard McNair entered in martial uniform; his lovely daughter, Christabetta on his arm.

Orange blossoms floating a diaphanous veil wreathed her head. The bridal dress was of white satin embroidered with seed pearls at the high neck and cuffs. Her beautiful dark eyes sought out the groom as she handed her fall bouquet to the maid-of-honor.

Christine was entranced by the service. "*To honor, to love, 'til death do us part,*" meant so much. These words emphasized a deep commitment of fidelity. She knew that she would expect the same vows from any prospective partner of hers.

Following the service, staff moved chairs to the outer walls and afternoon tea was served. The wedding party paraded up the winding staircase to the spacious second floor hall for photographs.

Of the eighty attendants, forty of them had been invited to the wedding supper. After numerous toasts, several meat courses, and deliciously prepared vegetables the wedding cake was ceremoniously borne in and placed before the radiant couple.

After dinner the ladies were presented with dance cards. Although Christine portrayed poise beyond her years, the young men buzzed around her, eager to partner her in a dance. Lieutenant Conners signed her card three times. The evening was ablaze – lit by many candles and lamps and perspiring faces – reddish from exertion and perhaps too much port.

Christine and the lieutenant danced the money musk and quadrille. But before the night's end they came together in the newly acclaimed waltz. *"You are certainly most fetching tonight, my dear,"* he whispered in her ear. She smiled and flushed. Just then the Duchess signaled to her. It had been a long and exciting day and she was tired. They accepted the lieutenant's offer to see them safely to their residence.

The ladies breakfasted at home, but were invited to lunch with Governor McNair and his wife in the great dining room.

"I'm to have a long week in court," remonstrated the governor. *"Conners, would you escort the Duchess and her companion? I'm sure they would find the sights about town most interesting!"*

"Of course sir, I would be most happy to" he responded and winked at Christine.

So, in the remaining days of their stay the threesome visited their host's new bank, the district courthouse, three new churches, and the railroad station. They stood on the mountain brow for a scenic panorama of Hamilton.

Although in the presence of a chaperone, Charles Conners flirted with and flattered both women. He usually caught Christine off guard and her cheeks would momentarily burn.

Late the last afternoon while the duchess slept, Christine decided to wander the beautiful grounds for the last time. She chose a short cut to the orchard through the stable yard. As she approached the coach house she heard a giggle – then a high-pitched laugh. The top double door of a nearby stall was open and she peered in. There in the straw, hair disheveled, blouse off the shoulder, was a kitchen maid. Her semi-clad companion was none other than Charles. She stepped back quickly, biting her tongue. She sought a quiet bench at the front of the grand estate – staring at the bay. *"Couldn't count on that lad for a commitment,"* she said aloud.

When the two met after lunch the next day, Charles asked if he could keep in touch with her by mail. Christine gave him a haughty look and refused. He then knew what she had seen. His parting comment: *"I thought you Scottish lassies came looking for husbands. I'm disappointed in you, Christine! Adieu!"* She knew a sharp and witty response would be wasted on such a man. So, head held high, she joined the Duchess.

Chapter 8
Two for Niagara

After a short lunch the ladies bade their host and hostess farewell. "*Thank you both for the invitation to join you for your family wedding,*" they said each in their own way: a Scottish burr and a melodic French. Sir Howard ordered a team to transport them. At a Hamilton wharf they booked on a small steamer that had recently arrived from Toronto. Niagara, with its now famous falls was the place to see. It was being eulogized by writers, poets, painters and photographers alike. They were not quite ready to try the new train running to Niagara. Although both had seen these iron horses in their respective countries, they wanted to talk to people who had ridden in them.

Their trip by steamboat was to take about an hour and a half, conditions being favorable. "*Whooo! Whooo!*" the whistle sounded and it chugged out of the harbor and into the deeper waters of the lake. They were required to stand on deck. They, and the six others moved about to exercise and enjoy the fall colors.

They were about an hour into the voyage. Suddenly from the engine room – a white-faced operator strode to the captain. He spoke in low tones: "*Sorry sir, we've a small fire below!*" He had hardly finished speaking when the machinist, enveloped in flames, tore up the stairs and dove into the water "*Catch the preserver*" his buddy shouted. Flames were climbing the stairs! The captain called, "*Lower the boats!*"

The machinist, rescued first was wrapped quickly in a blanket. Christine grasped the Duchess's arm and guided her into the safety of the first rescue craft. A young man assisted his new bride to a bench in the stern. Christine thought, "*Not an auspicious beginning to married life!*"

The stocky young seaman manned the oars. An off-shore wind was light and the craft, followed by the second, bearing the captain, an older couple and their two grandchildren, bore south toward a distant wharf.

As they were assisted to disembark, a tall figure rushed down the slope from the lakeside inn. "*Are you all right? I'm Stadler the innkeeper. I've been splitting wood and just saw your steamer go down!*"

They were shaken, but fairly dry and unharmed. All expressed their gratitude to the captain and his staff.

"The wife is preparing tea for you all," said their host as he assisted the elderly couple uphill toward the modest inn. *"We are at the mouth of 15 mile creek as measured from Niagara,"* he continued.

The small company was seated for the evening meal of squash, cabbage, mutton and boiled potatoes. Before dessert and ale, the captain rose to speak. *"Mr. Sadler's neighbor rescued the luggage most fortunately. I have arranged that Sadler will transport you to Niagara-on-the-Lake by skiff to-morrow morning. From there you may take a stage to the falls area. He'll make a second trip with the luggage. You must direct him. I have rewarded the rescuer."*

"How blessed we are that our gowns and night wear have been saved," shared Christine gratefully with the duchess. *"Oui, ma chère it is so! Shall we walk now?"* she requested. The inn was a comfortable walk to the macadamized lakeshore road. The fall air was fresh and the menacing insects had died off. When they returned to the inn they were invited to play

Whist. While they joined a table, the captain and the keeper set up a game of chess.

After an early morning breakfast the congenial group boarded Stadler's barque. They set off with a good prevailing breeze and were deposited within half an hour at the busy docks of Niagara-on-the-Lake. Christine spoke with the dock supervisor. "*Mr. Stadler will return with our luggage later. Would ye have it taken to Clifton House as soon as possible please?*"

All eight of the their party climbed aboard a waiting stagecoach. They were finally on the last lap of their journey to the famous falls. As Christine's diary reported: "*We passed Brock's Monument half-way. We followed the river and excitement grew. The horses tossed their heads higher and we too, heard a thunderous roar which grew immensely as we drew near. The atmosphere seemed at first like the Glasgow Carnival: bustling horse-drawn conveyances, noisy pedestrians on both sides of the road, hawkers peddling their wares: parasols, roasted chestnuts, cigars. The riverboat "Maid of the Mist" blew its whistle. We were there! We exited quickly to behold this fearful but marvelous sight: tons of water pouring in heavy but transparent sheets over a wide but sheer precipice of rock. Its roar and misty waters hypnotized the eight of us – and we stood transfixed for many minutes – speechless and frozen in time."*

Clifton House had been recommended by several of the Duchess's friends. It stood on a gentle rise opposite the falls. Its frontage was similar in width to the McNair estate of Hamilton. Three verandas circled the building; one per floor and four hundred guests could be accommodated. The large livery stable was located at the rear of the building. The Duchess had prearranged two adjoining front rooms on the third floor.

After a light lunch in the dining room, Christine busied herself unpacking her trunk. She looked out the window to view the falls on the American side. A gigantic wall of mist rose from the falls close by – dimming her view. *"I'll surely have to put cotton in my ears to sleep to-night,"* she said aloud, over the constant roar of water.

The bellboy delivered five letters. Two were for the Duchess. The remaining were for Christine. She opened the letter from her Father first. He claimed that he was well and that he had heard from her brother in Australia. He had been assigned the managership of a large sheep farm there. Laura Ross's message followed:

I have forwarded your Father's letter. I was given it by your housekeeper, Mrs. McKay. It would seem he has no knowledge of your difficulties at Bon Adventure.

Your Uncle Randolph seems to be in mourning. He only wears black; he continues to attend Kirk but walks with a stoop and barely looks up from the ground. He has petitioned me many times for your address – promising to try to make amends. I thought it right that your guardian be permitted to be in contact with you. He is your only relative in Canada, you know.

I have met a fine man who is in the shipping business in Oakdale. He is of a similar age and he has asked my permission to call. He is conducting the small Kirk choir and sings baritone handsomely.

Keep me advised of your activities.

I Remain Your Faithful Friend,

Laura

Waves of conflicting emotion swept over Christine as she held her Uncle's letter. She could not bring herself to open it right away. *"I'll save it 'til this evening after the Duchess is settled for the night,"* she half-heartedly promised herself.

The two ladies dressed for dinner. They joined the bustling humanity on the grand staircase, a crowd that was hungry and heading toward the gracious dining room. Lit candles made the glorious chandeliers sparkle. Young lads bore heavy food-laden platters. Older uniformed gentlemen served at the table. They ordered the whitefish dinner and learned that these were caught in the river below.

Their evening walk first took them westward along the river's edge to the great Falls of Niagara. The river's width above that mighty sheet of water amazed them. A nearby tourist pointed out the railway station on the American side. Trains had been bringing travelers to the site since 1841. Roebling, an engineer from the United States was in the process of completing a railway bridge to join the two countries. They could see that this bridge, lower down was almost completed. He had lost 60 of his work crew that very year to cholera.

It was after ten o'clock and Christine lit her oil lamp – dreading to open her Uncle's letter. It began:

My Dear Christine:

Thank you for opening this missive. I trust you are happy and well.

My days have darkened without your lovely and supportive presence here. Both Mrs. McKay and I walk in gloom and talk of the days of laughter and kindness. Do you recall Max, my setter bringing me my hat? Do you remember cook's strange dance on the wet floor my setters had left on a rainy day?

I am very busy, now insisting most appointments take place at home. I am in need of a younger partner and am beginning a search.

At this time, I have thought it best not to inform your Father of the situation. I have failed his trust in me to provide for you. A new Church of Scotland is being raised in Port Credit. I have sent him information pertaining – and I hope that he will apply for the new position and join us here in Canada. I hope this meets with your approval.

I ask your forgiveness for all that is past and pray that we may begin a happy relationship again. I speak with Reverend McClung weekly.

Penitently,

Your Uncle Randolph.

She slid the letter back into its envelope. Almost a month had passed since her angry departure. Herein she had been reminded of happy times. Having counseling sessions with a clergyman were important, too. And of great importance was that he was sorry for the past. Wanting to start afresh meant that he had nothing further to hide. She would have to make a careful response to his letter. "*Not tonight,*" she told herself – and headed for bed, emotionally exhausted.

The Duchess had planned to stay at the hotel for two weeks. They took advantage of a daily teatime at half past three in the large lounge. They took late afternoon walks along the river. The lower Niagara River had more beautiful surroundings: deeper forest and a larger variety of plants and birds. They would often stop on the bridge that led to the United States. Its construction had begun in 1851. It was now safe for horse and carriage traffic to cross. One day they hired a trap with driver and explored the American side. Their route took them past several mills that were utilizing the powerful river water.

One morning they decided to visit a museum a short walk from their residence. The Duchess had visited the world famous British Museum in London. For Christine this was a new experience. By the time the pair had inspected an Egyptian mummy with grave artifacts, water colors of very early Canada, native Indian items: arrowheads, moccasins, shirt, dress and pants beautifully beaded, and glassed in displays of butterflies, insects and stuffed animals, they were both very impressed by this new land.

Another day they visited "*The Reader*" a nearby bookshop. They browsed for nearly an hour. Christine purchased "Nicholas Nickleby" by Charles Dickens. Then they took their lunch at the pagoda-shaped tearoom next door.

While the Duchess rested the next afternoon, Christine walked to the dock where *"The Maid of the Mist"* a small tourist steamboat was anchored. She purchased a ticket. While she was buttoning an oil cloth coat, a young gentleman bowed to her and spoke with a familiar accent.

"Good day, Miss. I am Glen Andrews. I am studying geology at the University of Edinburgh. I've left my camera with the ticket agent. The pictures I have taken while here will provide for my thesis next fall. May I be so bold to ask yer name and what brings ye to this interesting place?". Christine introduced herself and explained her relationship with the Duchess and her position as her traveling companion. Their conversation touched on the Scottish clearances. They planned to meet again at week's end at the ball held at Clifton House. They were interrupted by the roar of the falls as the craft circled its foamy base.

It was Saturday evening. Christine and the duchess, dressed in their best glided into the music-filled ballroom. They took velvet chairs, pillar-side. After a short chat, several gentlemen lined up to sign their dance cards. It was early November and crisp outside. Indoors it was warm, the air heated by hundreds of candles in chandeliers, candelabra and three huge fireplaces. The ladies fanned their faces. Glen Andrews approached, handsomely dressed in formal wear, and signed her card in four places. The duchess conservatively allowed just six partners for the evening. During the orchestra's intermission, as they rested the duchess said. "*Ma chère Christine, I'm beginning to tire of your blue evening frock. We will see if there is a dress salon in the vicinity. A new one would be a treat for my eyes!*"

Mid-week the two decided to explore the Curiosity Shops. Irish girls paraded up and down in front of these warmly urging passersby to enter. "*Come ladies, enter to see the wares,*" they invited and held the door open for the pair. They spent over an hour in the first shop. It was larger and brighter than the second. It offered many interesting items to the tourist: coal-oil lamps, yard goods, hand-carved furniture and figurines from Quebec, candelabra, leather goods: belts, harness, candy of maple syrup, jewelry, china, shawls for infants and ladies, stools, chests, bird cages and much more. The duchess purchased a new burgundy shawl for herself and insisted that Christine have a cameo brooch she was quietly admiring.

Their sojourn was over. It was time to leave Niagara behind. The ports of Lake Ontario were still open but could start to be iced-in mid-November. They arrived in Niagara-on-the-Lake two hours before they were to board the steamship for Kingston. On the fashionable downtown main street they discovered a ladies' dress shop. The proprietress offered ten garments ready-made by her staff. The duchess insisted Christine try on a lovely rose taffeta gown. She declared, *"It's perfect for you!"* Realizing her wages would not permit such a luxury she responded humbly, *"Merci, I am sure!"*

Chapter 9
A New Man

They chugged out of Niagara-on-the-Lake Harbor aboard the steamship, *"La Reine"*. It was newer and larger than the one lost by fire. Christine strained to see Oakdale as they passed. Suddenly, in her mind's eye she saw Uncle Randolph and recalled his hearty laugh and twinkling eyes. She missed their fireside talks, rich with facts, ideas and opinions.

After Christine had left and had begun new adventures with Laura Ross and Duchess La Fleur, Uncle Randolph took to heart that "*whatever you sow, so shall you reap.*" As a result of his actions he had planted fear, distrust and disgust and he was deeply sorry.

One late afternoon he found himself at Tailor McKlintock's Shop. While he spoke to the proprietor, discussing the legal ramifications of a partnership, his eye caught sight of a lovely lady. She was sitting in the back corner of the shop quietly arranging feathers on a deep green felt hat. She occasionally looked their way. *"Is this Mrs. Reid whom I met at Kirk last week?"* he mused. He then remembered that he had heard that she had been tragically widowed.

They nodded to each other in acknowledgment. When Randolph's meeting concluded, Sylvia was ready to leave as well. She accepted his arm to help her navigate the boarded sidewalk that led to her cottage off the main street. Her father had been a professor of philosophy at Cambridge University and believed his daughter should be well educated. As they shared an interest in horses, music and art their friendship grew. It slowly blossomed into love. They sat together at Kirk, enjoyed a horse fair, and took long lakeside walks culminating at the port. They watched ships coming and going many Saturday afternoons. Plays and musicals entertained them. On Sundays, they accepted invitations to afternoon tea.

Randolph MacDonald also set up a fund to provide an education for young Stuart McKay. His Mother knew nothing of the past, but accepted the arrangement as a bonus for her long and faithful service as the lawyer's housekeeper.

MacDonald's legal firm expanded quickly as new residents arrived and necessary businesses opened. His crumbled self-esteem took on new strength, fed by the deep friendship and love offered by his gracious lady, Sylvia Reid. His happiness was evident in a light step, pleasant smile and warm greeting for everyone he met. He drew up wills and land deeds, formulated business partnerships and dealt in mortgages. He promised himself that Sunday would be his day of rest.

His responsibilities continued to increase. Before Christmas he was told by Reverend McClung that a young man he knew was due to graduate from a course of law, Edinburgh University. He was in his early twenties and wished to emigrate. *"Please give me his address,"* requested MacDonald. *"I'll write to offer a position and money for his passage."*

Chapter 10
Pre-Christmas Sojourn in Kingston

As the steamship bearing Christine and the Duchess approached Navy Bay and its intended wharf, the passengers noted a boat flying the naval ensign heading out to greet them. It's captain boarded and thoroughly checked their credentials (letters of introduction, calling or business cards, private correspondence) before allowing them to land at the naval base. The docks were alive with soldiers and sailors from Scotland and England – some working on schooner restoration while others were helping to finish details on a newly constructed steamboat. At the end of the bay workmen were putting up smaller craft in dry dock for the winter months. Many heads turned to admire the lovely young newcomer, Christine. The boldest gave her a wink as she passed.

Their crew began to unload the luggage and to place it on the dock. They heard the rapid pattern of horse's hooves and a shout "*Bienvenu, Janine, nous avon arrivés.*" Elise and husband, George, pulled the bay up short at the wharf's edge – and the two women ran into each other's arms. Janine had met Elise at her sister's home in Montreal some months before. They had quickly become fast friends. George managed the Bank of Montreal. They resided in a classic revival home – fronted by eight high windows, four on each side of an open porch with supported columns. The duration of the Duchess's visit would be influenced by the weather. The road to Montreal would have to be open to travel by sleigh.

When they had settled in, Christine began a letter to her uncle.

"Kingston, December, 1854

Dear Uncle Randolph,

We have traveled safely by steamboat from Niagara-on-the-Lake to Kingston. The Duchess plans to be in Montreal for Christmas and New Year's with her sister, Louise. At present we are staying with new friends of the Duchess, Elise and George Montgomery.

We have been invited to a dignitary's fifteenth wedding anniversary celebrations this weekend.

We hope to be given a tour of Fort Henry, the Naval Shipyards and the Rideau Canal.

Duchess La Fleur has announced that she has booked passage home to England mid-April. She will then no longer require my services.

May I please return to your residence? I am most able to translate from French to English when you may require it.

Sincerely,

Your Niece, Christine MacDonald"

With the help of the household's maid, Christine spent some time washing and pressing their wardrobes. Her eyes glowed as she unpacked her new rose taffeta gown.

The two visitors spent much of an afternoon in the city library, browsing the shelves and then reading newspapers in English and French from home and abroad. One evening the Montgomerys took them to the fashionable Wellington Arms Inn for a roast beef dinner.

The weekend arrived. The anniversary of Elizabeth and James Walker was to be celebrated at their country home six miles from the city. The duchess was representing her sister, Louise, and husband René. They could not attend because of a governmental appointment in Quebec City. The two ladies dressed in fresh supper gowns. A sleigh driven by a local hosteller arrived and the pair, Christine in her hooded greatcoat and the duchess in one of wolf, snuggled down under buffalo robes. Foot warmers in boxes at their feet added to their comfort. Before they knew it, they were being helped from the conveyance at a wonderful two storey red brick home. The snow sparkled about them and crunched at their step. Beyond the house – raised to the skies – branches of maple and spruce held splishes and splashes of spun snow. Christine paused to drink in creation. Then the duchess stamped her foot and reality won the moment.

The butler requested their wraps, and then introduced them to the family, lined up to receive guests. Beside Elizabeth and James stood the tall fair William, the son of twelve years. Beside him were his two sisters, hands clasped in front; Ann aged ten and Victoria seven. Seated quietly behind the children was their governess, Susan Morton, and she was introduced. The children, governess and the two ladies were led by the maid into the parlor. The Duchess was happy to be seated. The governess, sensing the children were very excited asked, "*William, girls, shall we take Miss MacDonald to see your classroom and playroom before tea?"* Their response was swift: *"Yes, oh yes, please!"*

"William, please ask your parents if we may be excused for a while."

Off the children skipped to the servant's back stairs, which led to the second floor. They first visited a bright whitewashed classroom – each child showing Christine where they sat at desk. When they arrived at their playroom, they organized a ball game rolling one to each other along the floor. Then they set up pins for bowling. Christine and Susan chatted.

"I've wanted to teach school since I was thirteen. Our Father provided daily studies 'til I left Scotland. Then Uncle Randolph requested help. Of course ye know of the period of "Clearances" in our country. And – here I am!"

"Your fine education would be valued here," added Susan. *"It still is a man's job to teach in a village or city school. If a woman marries she must stop teaching. So, I find being a governess in a large home most suitable for now. These positions are scarce here in the Canadas. I've been most fortunate to obtain this post. I attended a small girl's boarding school in England."*

Their friendly and informative conversation continued on. Christine was elated to have met someone of her own age to share some of her hopes and dreams. The children and the young ladies were summoned to the three o'clock reception. Dinner for twenty followed in the dining room.

Susan asked if she could share their ride back to the city. She had arranged to spend Saturday evening and Sunday at a friend's. Their former driver reappeared at nine o'clock. The three ladies thanked their hosts and settled under warm covers in the sleigh. Unnoticed by all three, the wind, from the north, had been at gale force all afternoon. It had subsided somewhat. About four miles into their late night journey it happened. The little horse hit a fallen tree, hidden by snow, and was thrown over by the impact casting sleigh, driver and occupants into snowdrifts at the roadside. Christine stood up first – checking her limbs – moving and stretching them. Then she moved quickly to assist the Duchess to her feet.

"Mon dieu, mon dieu," the duchess moaned. Her right shoulder was slightly sprained and she massaged it. Susan was assisted to her feet by the driver. She had been

thrown further and as she brushed snow off her skirt they heard the jangle of sleigh bells. A few moments later a second sleigh pulled up short and just in time. Two military men rushed to the disheveled party. Susan had met Captain Thomas Whitson previously at the Church of England. Her blush was hidden by the dark of the night. *"We've just been visiting friends at the Naval Base. This is Lieutenant Bernard Kent,"* added the captain.

"We are heading to barracks at the fort. May we convey you to your residences, ladies?" asked the lieutenant. As they settled in the landau, a third sled arrived. The young privates of the captain's platoon were commanded to clear the important road of the fallen tree. About a quarter of a mile from the accident scene, a sharp, startling crack of a gun sliced the air. The sturdy little horse, unable to rise again had been dispatched. Christine's eyes immediately filled with tears. Only Bernard Kent noticed those two trails on her cheeks.

Before the ladies were deposited safely at their locations, Susan asked Christine to accompany her to morning service the following day. Christine obtained the Duchess's permission and walked to the church a few blocks away. There there met the two rescuers, respectable young men.

"Would you like a tour of Fort Henry and the Naval Base?" Captain Whitson asked. *"My friend and I have been posted in Kingston for two years, so we know it well. Would Wednesday be a good day for you both?"*

"We would have to request a free day from our employers. Would the Duchess be our chaperone, do you think Christine?" Susan responded quickly – most willing to be in the captain's company again.

The plans were accepted. They arrived at the fort entrance and freed themselves of the travel robes while the two gentlemen announced the party at the guardhouse. They climbed up and over earthworks on their path to the main barracks. Many of the large guns were pointed north to engage an enemy approaching overland. They were led briskly to an upper room. A new invention, the Addison stove, was a marvel. It could heat cannon balls. These would be fired at enemy craft attacking the fort from the water. They were expected to start a fire on board. They heard the swirl of bagpipes and returned to the parade area. Christine's heart thrilled to the sound and her thoughts were drawn back momentarily to Scotland. Two pipers in kilts led a platoon of Scots up the centre. They were followed by a scarlet-jacketed English group – played along by the fife and drums. Lieutenant Kent explained that Welsh Fusiliers had manned this fort in the 1840's.

"Could ye tell us about the towers we saw along the waterfront as we landed in the city?" asked Christine.

"There were eight towers built in 1845 to secure the waterfront. The largest Martello tower is called the Fort Frederick Tower. It has a drawbridge and has thirty-two pound carronades, short cannons mounted," offered Captain Whitson.

The party took lunch at the King's Table Inn. Christine knew that Jacques, their unfortunate driver was employed there. As they were about to leave she excused herself to present an envelope to the owner. She had enclosed two pounds to help Jacques purchase a new horse.

Their next stop was the Naval Base. They were refused entrance. The gatekeeper explained that a rush was on to get work completed before heavy snow arrived and extreme cold set in. The two ladies, Christine and Janine had disembarked there on arrival, so accepted the change of plans easily.

The final goal of the day was to see the Rideau Canal completed in 1835. It was closed for the season, but they could observe one of the locks. Their two military companions shared much information. It was considered to be the greatest engineering feat of the century. There were twenty-four dams and forty-six locks between Kingston on Lake Ontario and Bytown on the Ottawa River. It was built virtually by hand and many workers had lost their lives. It provided a secure supply route between Montreal on the St. Lawrence River and The Great Lakes should an attack be launched again from the United States. After a walk about through snow, they returned to the landau. The horses were stamping and snorting in the cold air and took them off at a smart pace.

All five had received invitations to a ball to be held at the Walker's country residence the following weekend. The Duchess had caught a cold and declined to attend, but insisted Christine go under the watchful eye of her hosts. Janine insisted that Christine wear her wolf coat over her rose taffeta gown. She clicked her tongue as she fastened a silk rose to Christine's hair. "*Belle, belle! She does not know how lovely she looks!*" she thought.

The Walkers provided her transportation. She presented the duchess's note to her hosts and joined Susan who was conversing with Captain Whitson. Susan was flushing and fanning her face with a beautifully embroidered fan. Susan stretched out her hand in welcome, then placed a dance card in it. Whitson allowed his friend Kent only one dance with Susan. His monopoly meant only one thing – they were mutually attracted – and even in love. Christine's card filled quickly. The two young officers were the Walker's favorites, but there were other young men present: bankers, merchants and municipal officers. Bernard Kent signed Christine's card for four dances early. They both favored the waltz, newly introduced from Europe. The music was provided by members of the British Military stationed at the fort.

Two letters arrived for Christine early in the week. She read Laura's first. Her friend expressed her increased attraction for Joseph, her new admirer. She also emphasized that her

Uncle Randolph had changed dramatically. He was more dapper in dress and happier in countenance. Christine then opened her uncle's correspondence and read:

Bon Adventure

Oakdale, December, 1854

My Dear Christine,

I have such good news to report!

Firstly I have met a wonderful woman, Sylvia Reid. We were introduced at Kirk. Her husband was killed in an accident five years ago at the shipbuilding yard. He was a partner in the business and is sorely missed. She has an excellent education and a most lovely demeanor. We have become very good friends and care for each other deeply. I have asked for her hand in marriage. She accepted and our plan is to be joined together in June.

Secondly, I have sent a ship's fare to a young law graduate, Graham Sutherland. He will leave Scotland in April to join me in my law office.

Finally, I await your Father's letter in connection with serving the Port Credit Kirk here in Canada.

Of course, my dear you may return to your Uncle's home! I have had occasion to require the services of a translator of French.

I Remain Your Devoted Uncle,

Randolph MacDonald.

Chapter 11
December in Montreal

Christine made arrangements with a busy coaching station for a one-way trip to Montreal for two. The roads were snow packed and firm so that a sleigh could make good time. Elise and the Duchess parted reluctantly, but promised to correspond.

The large wooden curved-back sleigh had a box to hold luggage. The four travelers, for they were joined by a middle-aged couple going to Cornwall, snuggled down under buffalo robes while their feet searched for the warmers.

Their route took them along the St. Lawrence River – quiet now and iced in near shore. They observed piles of railway ties, snow covered and embankments ready for rails. Every fifteen to twenty miles they stopped for a change of horses. Conditions were good and they traveled about ten miles per hour. When they reached a stop the horses' nostrils were frosted in white.

Christine's diary listed Gananoque, Mallorytown and an overnight stay in Brockville. A light snow began to fall the second morning. They met several sleighs and farmers' sleds traveling in the opposite direction. "*Hellos*" were accompanied by vigorous waves from all travelers. Sleigh bells jangling, they sped through Prescott, Cardinal and Iroquois. The approach of darkness and the increased snowfall forced an over-night stop in Morrisburg. Guy, their driver spent the evening carousing with friends at the Bear's Inn. The next morning passengers found him "*like a bear with a sore head.*" Fortunately he had strong hands for the reins. The Foresters, their traveling companions were very happy when they arrived safely in Cornwall. There the two ladies spent their third night, this time in a new inn. They were relieved that a different driver was to complete their trip. He told them that the Grand Trunk Railway service from Toronto to Montreal should be ready by the fall of 1856. When they reached Dorion they knew they were in Lower Canada. On through Chateauguay, they sped across a bridge, at last they were on the Island of Montreal.

The city's population was about sixty thousand at this time and both ladies looked forward expectantly to their arrival. The owner of a posting station at the outskirts promised them a safe delivery to the Langevin residence.

They were enthused by the several miles of travel within the city. When they reached Rue Saint Dominique they turned north three miles 'til they reached the estate property of the Langevins, Louise and René. It was late afternoon. The butler, Pierre and the maid, Emilie bowed and curtseyed at their introduction. Pierre announced that le petit dejeuner (breakfast) was at eight o'clock. Lunch hour could vary, but le diner was precisely at seven in the evening. Christine unpacked the Duchess's wardrobe. When they arrived, Brigitte, their cook had been busy. At the appointed hour a delicious meal of venison and vegetables was presented and followed by her wonderful pumpkin pie. *"Our son, Jules is at university studying law, but he will be home to celebrate Christmas and New Year's,"* explained René as they left the table.

"We'll sit in the parlor now," invited Louise, taking her sister's arm. *"René will enjoy his pipe in the office."* The hostess assured Christine that she was welcome to join them. Christine excused herself to retrieve needlework, pillowcases that she was working as a Christmas gift for her host family.

René had announced earlier that a party to welcome Janine was set for the Saturday following. Completely immersed in the French language now, Christine looked forward to learning more before the event arrived. She, too, had made friends with their beautiful black bouvier, Roi (King). They had taken many long walks together within the estate grounds. René was pleased to hand his leash to her. He was extremely busy as it was year-end in his wine importing business. He also held a government position in the Ministry of Trade.

Party day arrived. Everyone's excitement was palpable. The ladies had agreed not to wear gowns of identical material for special occasions. So Janine chose a navy velvet and Christine her new rose taffeta.

The guests arrived about a quarter after six to meet the duchess, the guest of honor, and to sip an aperitif. Christine was introduced as a chère amie (dear friend). A superb meal was served by Pierre and Emilie. Bottles of red wine from René's cellar were opened and left on the table. Pork medallions were surrounded by baked apple. Kale and carrots were the hot vegetables. The salad was a mild sauerkraut, a recipe Brigitte had begged from a German friend. A sweet soufflé was followed by a choice of liqueurs. Coffee, a new and expensive drink, was served in mini-cups in the parlor.

Many of the people Janine met that evening were musicians, fellow admirers of her sister Louise, who was a classically trained violinist. Evangeline was a chanteuse (singer) of note. Marielle played the flute, Sophie the piano. The small ensemble provided the beautiful music of Mozart and Brahms and the lesser known French composers, Alkan and Dancla. Toward the end of the evening, Evangeline sang French Canadian folk songs and invited her audience to participate.

As the melody of the last chorus of "*Un Canadien Errant*" filled the air, everyone felt a cold draft and heard the clump of feet. The French doors of the parlor flew open. "*Bon soir, ma mere et mon pere!*" a young man shouted, then staggered up the winding staircase, hopefully to bed. Christine's eyes met the duchess's and she guessed. "*So this is Jules – hmm!*" From the corner of the room René responded: "*These young students, you know, - and it's Saturday night.*" And Christine was quite surprised at this accepting attitude. His guests had been rudely interrupted and he had been greeted most impolitely.

Preparations for Christmas began. Christine finished embroidering a set of three handkerchiefs for the duchess. The pillowcases were completed. The duchess purchased elbow length evening gloves for Christine. Pierre brought in cedar from the countryside. It made wonderful garlands to decorate the grand staircase, fireplaces and front entrance, and filled the place with a unique fragrance. The house was lit by gas lamps now. Yet Brigitte purchased a dozen red candles to add to the festiveness. At the same market she found a gigantic goose for the Christmas table. Christmas Eve Christine heard laughter and sneezing coming from the kitchen. As she opened the door – what a sight! Brigitte and Emilie were almost lost in a cloud of white feathers.

That evening the family's custom was to attend Mass. They reached Notre Dame Basilica in the Place d'Armes at ten thirty. Christine watched carefully and followed the special rituals. The boys' choir filled the chancel with "*Silent Night.*" On their return they met many sleighs, phaetons, and sleds on the roads, some returning from church, others from merry-making with friends and family.

The hearty Christmas meal was served at noon. Brigitte's prize goose arrived on a large platter and oozed juices. Large rosy baked apples surrounded it. René proposed many toasts.

Then they retired to the parlor to exchange gifts. The household staff was invited to join the family and their guests. They stood together and René called each one to him to receive a money gift. The recipients of Christine's needlework were very pleased. Beside the gloves from Janine and a soft blue woolen shawl from Louise, Christine opened a gift that surprised her. A lovely white reticule, a bag for evening of silk and embroidered with pastel flowers, was a gift from Jules. She had not thought of a gift for him and felt overwhelmed.

Later that afternoon, the Duchess at the piano and Louise on the violin played the family's seasonal favorites. The musicale lasted an hour, then they dispersed. Christine offered to take Roi (the bouvier) for a walk and Jules jumped at the chance to accompany her. They spoke in both French and English as they tramped through the grounds.

Christine, the newcomer, had many questions for Jules: *"Is this your first meeting with your aunt? When was the Basilica built? When was the Lachine Canal built and for what purpose?"* His answers satisfied and impressed her. *"This is the second time Aunt Janine has visited. Notre Dame Basilica was completed in 1829 and the Canal in 1824 so that boats could escape the rapids."* Then, he added, *"And did you like my gift?"* As she responded in the affirmative, she realized that it had put a little hook into her. *"What is his motive?"* she wondered.

Greetings of the Season had arrived by mail from several people: Christine's father, her Uncle Randolph, and her friends Laura Ross and Susan Morton. Susan shared new information, but not unexpected: she was to be officially engaged to Captain Whitson, Christmas Eve.

Two days after Christmas, Emilie received word that her Mother was ill. She requested leave to go home to help. There were four younger children needing care. Christine offered to help with the children while Emilie cared for her Mother.

Christine and Emilie arrived at a simple habitant home. The outer structure was of wood planks, well seasoned to gray tones by the elements. The roof was sharp to handle a winter's snow. The heavy outer door swung open to reveal the interior. A smooth pine table dominated the dark room. Around it, seated on high-back wicker chairs, the four children sat quietly playing with wooden blocks. "*What are you making, children?*" Christine asked in French. They replied in chorus, "*Un chateau pour Maman.*"

The girls visited daily, prepared meals, did laundry and amused the children while the cholera-stricken woman recuperated. Fortunately she was strong and her body was fighting off the disease remarkably well. Brigitte had sent hearty soups for the whole family. The disease was most prevalent in the Irish section of the city called Griffintown. Doctors were suggesting that all drinking water be boiled. Christine returned to the estate at the end of the week to attend to the Duchess's wardrobe requirements and assist with her post Christmas correspondence. Janine had missed her pleasant companion and hugged her on her return.

Chapter 12
Montreal in January

Duchess La Fleur knew that Christine had worked very hard the past few days. Often when she was caught with a distant look in her eyes she would admit she was thinking of her father at home in Scotland, or her Uncle Randolph. Janine had learned that the Scots celebrated New Year's or Hogmanay in a special way. Christine had met the McTavishes, Sarah and Joshua, at the duchess's welcoming party. She encouraged Christine to accept their invitation to spend a few days with them around this event. Christine was tempted to remain at home when she was told that she would miss French Canadian seasonal treats: tortière and sugar pie. But she yearned to celebrate the Scottish way.

Helen, the McTavish's seventeen-year-old daughter came for Christine in the family's cariole. They chatted as they drove to the large Georgian home. It was located in the area of Montreal mostly settled by the British and called West Mount. *"I'm studying Literature, Latin and Bible with Reverend McCready"* Helen offered. She added, *"You certainly have become proficient in French. I'm sure this would help you to obtain a teaching post."* Helen admired Christine for immigrating alone. She hoped that they would become good friends.

The girls became more acquainted as they took meals together, sang of an evening, walked the family's retriever, or embroidered or painted in watercolors of an afternoon.

The night of the celebration arrived. Christine decided that her MacDonald tartan plaid that she had received from her Father at Christmas would be the best match for her deep blue silk gown. She threw the scarf (red touched with green) over her shoulder and pinned it securely at her waist. Helen had chosen a peach taffeta ball gown. She called at Christine's door and the two young ladies, eyes sparkling in anticipation, glided gracefully down the circular staircase and into the drawing room already buzzing with people. The men stood about talking and sipping wine. They were resplendent in velvet jackets and white frilly shirts, and wore kilts of their clan's tartan adorned with a sporran hanging from their belts. Their long socks were to the knees and their black shoes were of soft leather.

The ladies intermingled. Their ball gowns were of marvelous colors and materials:

silks, velvets and taffetas. And each wore the plaid. Helen took Christine by the arm, graciously introducing her to many of her friends. When they reached a small group of Scottish soldiers of the 71st Highland Regiment, the men became silent as they noted the two beauties approaching. Lieutenant Matthew Campbell was immediately attracted to Christine. They both had blue eyes and fair hair. He quickly requested that she partner with him for the first dance.

Before midnight a short program was presented. The Highland Fling, a folk dance was performed by the two young daughters of the McFee family. To prepare for the Sword Dance, two sets of two swords were placed in cross formation on the floor. The company stood in awe. Two young soldiers, feet shod in soft black slippers, leaped to the centre and then out to the music of the bagpipes. Not a slipper was cut – and the spectators gave the dancers hearty applause.

The grandfather clock began to strike twelve. As the last gong chimed, a loud knock echoed from the wooden front door. One of the party answered it.

A spritely dark-haired middle-aged man entered. He bore a basket containing bread, representing food, coal which could provide heat and warmth, and wine to insure friendship. This ritual of FIRST FOOTING would guarantee a beneficent year to all present in the house. He was heartily applauded and thanked.

Mr. McTavish then called the company to prayer "*Our Father,*" he began "*we thank you for the blessings of the past year. We ask for continued prosperity in the year to come. Bless this food and our fellowship together. Amen.*" The butler led the assemblage into the dining room where the buffet was set with fish, game, cold cuts, breads, scones and pickled vegetables. A side table held many servings of plum and carrot puddings and decanters of whiskey. As they finished their past midnight meal, they were invited by their host to participate in several toasts. As McTavish raised his glass, he declared: "*To the New Year 1855 ...to Bonny Scotland ...to our new country, Canada ...to Queen Victoria and Prince Albert ...and to all the beautiful ladies present.*" And the male voices responded, "*Here! Here!*" and tilted their glasses.

After a gift exchange, a small military orchestra formed in one corner. Two flutists and violinists, a harpist, and a pianist rendered a few songs of Scotland, some by Robert Burns. Then the dance music began and Matthew claimed Christine as his partner. The skirl of the pipes and the whirl of the tartans of the Robertsons, Murrays, MacLennans and others filled the room. Christine felt exhilarated and at the same time proud and secure. Scotland was here too at this moment. They danced the schottische, reels and strathspeys to the tunes of "*The Marquis of Huntly's Farewell,*" "*Mary George's Daughter*" and others.

At party's end, the company stood in a large circle holding hands. Mr. McTavish, in his deep bass began "*Auld Lang Syne*", joined by the group. Christine had not accepted another partner all evening. And she was most lovely in the eyes of the young soldier. He asked, "*May I have yer permission to call and walk out with ye of a Sunday?*" Christine gave him the Duchess La Fleur's card and suggested that he ask her employer's permission. They parted, happy to know that they would likely meet again soon.

While Jules was away at university, he planned to see more of Christine. And so, he returned home each weekend to cherchez la femme. On occasion she saw him cornering a maid on the second floor. One Saturday afternoon Christine quietly stood at the top of the stairs, holding on to the rails. Jules stepped quickly out of the shadows and grasped her waist. She whirled around swiftly, elbows out and dealt him a solid blow in the ribs. She rushed downstairs to join Louise and the Duchess in the parlor. Recently she had been a victim of his nasty teasing at the table. And now this incident caused her to begin to fear him. As she prepared the Duchess for retirement she shared her experience. "*I've had quite enough of this young man's foolery!*" she emphasized. "*I know Jules is your nephew, Mademoiselle. I'm sorry but I can take no more!*" Tears began to fall as she continued, "*Would you be so kind to speak to him on my behalf? I would so appreciate it!*"

Sunday afternoon while Christine, Helen and Sarah McTavish were out walking with Matthew, Janine confronted her brazen nephew. "*What's this I hear? Manhandling Christine? There will be no more of it – do you understand? She has another interest, and it's not you! Bear it like a man!*" He had not felt the sharpness of his aunt's tongue before.

Admonished he left the room without a word. He hoped that his parents would not hear of it or his ample allowance might be cancelled. This would mean no partying with his fellow students. He needed to tread carefully and find another more willing to amuse him.

The third weekend arrived. Matthew had made plans for an outdoor activity. His pay and allowance from home allowed him to rent a sleigh for the party, Christine, Louise, and the Duchess. He surprised Christine by driving them to Place d'Armes where a sleigh race was scheduled. Participants were to line up at the south side of the square. At the crack of the starter's pistol they were to circumnavigate the square five times. Spectators' sleds and conveyances were drawn up on the four corners to be out of harm's way. Crack! Off they went! Fresh snow flew up off swift horses' hooves. Corners had to be taken carefully for a spill could cause disaster and cancel the race. Of the four starting teams, two were neck and neck on the home stretch. A phaeton, drawn by a matched team of blacks crossed the finish line first. Its red-faced young driver bowed first to his competitor, then to the crowd. When he dismounted he was presented a prize of five pounds.

The twenty-fifth of January was Robbie Burns' birthday. Scots around the world celebrated the bard's day. Christine was invited again to the McTavish home. She looked forward to seeing Helen again. Her eyes sparkled as she thought of seeing Matthew too.

The evening began with the Selkirk Grace, recited by McTavish. The company stood as the haggis, surrounded by heeps (turnips) and tatties (potatoes), was born on a platter and piped to the head of the table. The haggis was addressed, and toasts offered. A recitation of Burn's poems followed: "*My Luve is Like a Red Red Rose,*" "*To a Mouse,*" "*A Man's a Man for A' That.*" To end an interesting soirée, they sang his compositions heartily: "*Scots Wha Hae*" and "*Auld Lang Syne.*"

Three sleighs had brought the celebrants from the barracks. The captain assured the McTavishes that Miss MacDonald would be conveyed home safely. It was while under the buffalo robes that Matthew gently kissed her. His blue eyes glowed yet were tender. And, as she snuggled into his left side, his arm circled her shoulder. "*This is a little bit of Heaven,*" she thought.

Chapter 13
Montreal – February and March

Sunday became Christine's free day. She met Matthew and the McTavishes weekly and they were invited to lunch with the family. They met at St. Paul's Presbyterian Church on Rue Ste. Hélène. Interestingly it was owned by John Redpath and Peter McGill. Mid-February the family organized an afternoon toboggan party at Mount Royal. The sleighs, bells jangling bore the young people and chaperones to the area near Beaver Lake. From there it was uphill to the summit. They had so much fun as four crowded on the toboggan to slide down. A crackling bonfire safely located, provided a spot to warm hands. A piping hot cup of tea was available from an attendant, for tuppence.

The week following, the Duchess requested transportation to the lower part of Montreal near the river. A cariole with its hood up was driven to the entrance and Christine and the Duchess drew up the robes. As they sped down Rue St. Dominique toward the harbor, the charred remains of homes and large open spaces caused by the major fire of 1852 were still evident. *"Imagine twelve hundred homes destroyed here – and nine thousand people homeless,"* the Duchess moaned.

"And this was just three years ago!" Christine added. They were told that the city government required that the new homes be rebuilt in stone, not wood as in the past.

The driver turned westward along Rue la Commerce. They passed two sleds loaded with firewood. At the reins were the men called bucherons (lumbermen). The ladies commented on the off white blanket jackets they wore and noted the colorful sashes looped once at the waist. They knew that a blue tuque meant the habitant was of the Montreal area, while a red one meant he was from Quebec City. They soon reached the Bonsecours Market, now the City Hall. Many sleighs were releasing passengers there. Men wore their tall black beaver hats, the women their warm winter bonnets. The ladies took lunch at a small inn off the main route. The menu offered piping hot pea soup and crêpes. When they were refreshed, the Duchess requested their driver to portez them to the chapel called Notre Dame de Bon Secours, along the waterfront. There they alighted, not just to view the building, but also to have a time of reflection.

This beautiful chapel at the bottom of St. Paul Street was of distinctive architecture. Its two lovely grey turrets were on either side of a high central spire. The stone used in its construction was somber, but gas lamps and candles in candelabra gave a soft warm glow to the chancel. It was a bit warmer inside – but not warm enough that the ladies could remove their coats. The Duchess and Christine covered their heads and proceeded down the centre aisle of the nave to the third row of seats. Christine sat quietly while the Duchess went reverently to her knees. They remained silent and contemplative for some time. A Grey Nun entered from the right of the chancel and began to attend to the candles. They rose and approached her. The Duchess asked, "*When was the church built and who founded it?*" She answered politely, almost in a whisper, "*This beautiful edifice, built to the honor of Mother Mary was finished in 1675 by the encouragement of a teacher and nun, Marguerite Bourgeoys. It has been called the sailors' church since so many have come from their boats directly here to give thanks for a safe voyage.*" They thanked her. After a short conversation and the presentation of a money gift for the poor, the two found their transportation at the entrance door.

On the last weekend of February, Helen was to celebrate her eighteenth birthday. She chose to hold her party Saturday evening. Christine received permission to attend the special supper and to stay over-night. After they had eaten a delicious meal of chicken and dumplings, the young people prepared for the outdoors. Mr. McTavish hired an extra sleigh. The vehicles quickly filled with the happy partygoers who were dressed in bulky outer wear and who carried snowshoes. It was a clear, cold night. The snow sparkled in the light of a full moon. They glimpsed the red orange of a bonfire some distance ahead in the Mount Royal Park. They poured off the sleighs and sat on rough, wooden benches to attach their snowshoes to their winter boots. Matthew helped Christine to fasten hers and assisted her to her feet. They both lit a torch from the fire and followed McTavish along a trail that had been prepared by others earlier that day.

The man stoking the fire was fascinated by what he saw. A hypnotizing sight it was: the alternate glow of flickering torches weaving, as though without bearers, in and out along the circuitous trail. On the path, silence gradually fell on the group as they listened to the sound of their shoes in the snow and beheld the night sky spangled with stars. After a half hour trek, McTavish led his youthful followers back to the bonfire. Another attendant filled mighty mugs with tea and the steam rose from each cup into the crisp night air. Christine was grateful for the loan of the Duchess's hooded wolf coat. "*But you must keep warm and well,*" fussed the Duchess as Christine had left for the celebration.

The calendar indicated it was the first week of March. The Duchess made a special request. "*I would like to go to the old part of the city to buy a few treasures to take home to England from the Canadas.*" Thursday was the day set. The sleigh was needed especially after Wednesday's significant snowfall. They asked their driver to take them on a different route so that they might see more of the city. Off Rue Saint Dominique they turned west on Rue Sainte Catherine then south on Côte du Beaver Hall and to the art gallery recommended by the McTavishes. It had been established in 1847 on Great St. James Street by a group of artists. Krieghoff, one of the founders, had painted many scenes around Montreal before moving to Quebec City. The Duchess spent an hour absorbing the works. She then decided to purchase three Krieghoff prints: "*Place d'Armes a Montreal,"* *"French Canadian Habitants Playing at Cards,"* and *"Indians and Squaws of Lower Canada."* They would be safer to take back to England than framed pictures.

During the past few weeks letters had arrived for Christine. Her Uncle Randolph wrote: *"I look forward to the month of April with the arrival of my niece and my young Scottish assistant."* Laura Ross was still enamored by her new beau. Susan Morton announced, *"I'm to marry Captain Whitson in July. Would you consider being my attendant at the service, Christine?"* Of course Christine responded in the affirmative, hoping she would gain her uncle's permission for a trip to Kingston. Reverend MacDonald writing from Glasgow confirmed: *"I have accepted the position of minister to the Presbyterian Church in Port Credit. Margaret, my housekeeper has kin in the Canadas and would like to continue her service to me. She will accompany me on my journey in May."*

But her most recent correspondence was from Matthew. She read:

"My Dear Christine,

I am sorry to have to inform you that I will be posted to Halifax Citadel early April. It seems that there is increased American naval activity off Halifax Harbor. They require twenty-five of our best to augment the garrison.

I hope that we may correspond. I await your response.

In affectionate Regard,

Matthew"

"*Oh dear,*" she lamented, "*We've been getting on so well!*" Warm tears slid down her cheeks. They had enjoyed so many good times together.

Mid-March Emilie's family was going to be involved in sugaring-off: the collecting and processing of maple tree sap. The Duchess had enjoyed the sweet syrup on many a crêpe and wanted to observe the process. This was arranged. Christine and Janine were driven two miles north of the estate to an area heavily forested with maples. Their sleigh met a large sled driven by Emilie's father. Her brother, also aboard settled the two ladies on a low bench. They followed a lumber road to a wooden lean-to where a large wood fire crackled and spit. A blue tuqued habitant was stoking the fire while the other poured clear liquid from a pail into the huge black iron pot suspended over the open flames. "*As you see, Mademoiselle,*" said one of the men, "*we have hammered sharp, hollow wooden spikes into the trees. My boy with his dog and small sled collect the sap when each pail is full.*" On a plank supported by two wooden horses, eight rectangular wooden bowls were neatly arranged. "*My wife is cooling some of the liquid into sugar blocks which we will sell,*" continued the man who seemed in charge of the operation. A lady in a warm coat and scarf ladled the hot semi-liquid quickly into each container and steam rose into the air. "*I wish to order a large jug of your syrup to be sent to the Langevin estate,*" said the Duchess, reaching into her reticule to make the necessary payment. It was agreed that Emilie would bring the purchase to the kitchen when it was ready.

As they made their way home, a sled driven by a 71st Highlander sped past them. The two hunters aboard were hauling the carcass of a deer either to the barracks or to the lower city market. They neared the estate. A conveyance approached at a slower pace. A sturdy black horse was doing his best handling a heavy load of ice blocks. Christine was grateful that its owner was good-natured. As they passed she heard the driver clucking "*Bon, mon petit, bon bon!*"

Chapter 14
April – Good-Byes and Hellos

April arrived alternating showers and sunshine. Christine felt much in tune with nature for she was about to part with two people she cared for. Yet, she looked forward happily to seeing her Uncle Randolph and friend Laura Ross once again.

The McTavishes invited Christine to a farewell party for Matthew and three other young men who had been transferred to Nova Scotia. Their cook was able to purchase a large catch of salmon for the parting meal. The musicians did their best to keep the tunes light and joyful. Joshua McTavish and his wife, Sarah led the group to dance. They did the schottische and reels, ending with several Strauss waltzes to slow the pace. Christine and Matthew made a handsome couple – she blossoming in her rose taffeta and he sharp in his dress uniform. Sideline observers were heard to sigh, "*What a shame those two must part.*" Christine had kept her composure through the evening. But it was during the final circle where friends and family sang "*Auld Lang Syne*" that tears silently wet her cheeks.

Duchess La Fleur agreed to act as chaperone when Christine requested permission to say good-bye to Matthew. He was to board the steamer *"John Munn"* at the Jacques Cartier Pier. The dockside was bustling with activity: workers, travelers, luggage carts, boxes and barrels being moved by horse-drawn vehicles. The Scots marched to the wharf – kits carried on their backs. Their additional luggage followed in three simple carts. The McTavishes who had entertained and temporarily parented a number of the young men were at the wharf too. Helen waved to Christine. Christine returned the gesture but since time was of the essence, she was intent on finding Matthew in the crowd. The men were temporarily dismissed. Christine and Matthew met – neither speaking. Then Christine quietly presented him with two beautifully finished handkerchiefs bearing his initials M.C. *"Thank ye, my dear Christine,"* said Matthew, *"I'll treasure these always. Now I have a wee gift for ye."* Christine's eyes widened. Here in this little box she discovered a brooch. It was fashioned in silver, thistle in shape and centred with a dark green stone. *"I thought this would look well on yer plaid,"* he remarked. Christine thanked him and held his hand a little longer than propriety allowed. *"I shall surely treasure this,"* she continued, caressing the little box. The best that they could do now was to agree to correspond. Christine gave Matthew her uncle's address in Oakdale. The first mate blew the boat whistle to indicate that passengers should board. The Scottish captain re-grouped his men, marched them up the gangway and into the belly of the steamer, *"John Munn"*.

Christine would not have much time to mourn their parting. Both she and the Duchess must be prepared for travel. There was much washing, pressing, polishing of shoes and boots, then packing to do. And there were letters of thanks to be written in English for the Duchess to Sir Howard McNair and her hosts in Kingston, the Walkers. One afternoon as Christine prepared the Duchess's wardrobe for the second steamer trunk, she noticed stains on the Duchess's long white evening gloves. One was of red wine – planted by a middle-aged man in his cups. The other was dark and waxy – left by a gentleman who had recently colored his moustache. Christine was quietly amused as she removed the evidence.

Wednesday arrived. It was the day of the Duchess's departure. Christine rushed to pack her last minute items in a carpetbag which could be carried by hand.

Christine had a few minutes alone with her. They embraced, teary-eyed. Christine presented her with neatly wrapped gifts. The first contained woodcarvings of a habitant man and woman. The second present was a scarf of lace for her head, crocheted by Emilie's mother. It was to cover her head in holy places. "*Merci, merci, ma chère,*" purred the Duchess. "*Maintenant, I wish to leave you my wolf coat. I will not need it in mild English winters. It will remind you of me.*" Christine could hardly believe this. "*I must be dreaming,*" she thought. But her voice said, "*Oh, many, many thanks! You have been so kind to me during our time together. God bless you!*"

The Langevin's landau, pulled by prancing blacks bore the party and luggage to the Jacques Cartier wharf. The steamer *"Quebec"* was loading. The family expressed sadness but wished her "*Bon voyage.*" Christine shamelessly embraced Janine. They promised to write to each other in French.

Christine was scheduled to leave Montreal the following day. She now needed a trunk for the additional dress and coat that she had received. The Langevins provided one they no longer needed. Christine gave gifts as a thank you. Louise was pleased with the mantilla like that of Janine's. Her husband, Rene was grateful for a new hickory pipe.

The Langevins and Christine traveled by landau to the Alexander Pier. She would be journeying alone again so would have to be sharp and alert. *"Perhaps I might find some congenial lady aboard,"* she hoped. The steamboat, *"Free Trader"* whistled its departure. Christine stood clasping the rail and waving to the family below. The boat turned gently westward to head through the Lachine Canal.

As they chugged on their way, Christine had a few regrets. She would miss ice-skating on this very canal in dead of winter. On a couple of occasions when she was visiting the McTavishes for the weekend, the Langevins had watched ice-boat races on the Lachine. Other Saturday nights the Duchess and Louise had attended concerts and plays in the theatres of Montreal. *"Perhaps I'll visit again,"* she hoped. How could she not admire the spring hardwood forests lining the route? The soft yellow green stood out against a background of dark evergreens.

From the water she began to view some of the towns she had passed through last November by sleigh. Christine recalled Iroquois, Cardinal, Prescott and her over-night in Morrisburg. When they stopped for passengers in Kingston, a jolly middle-aged woman and her daughter boarded traveling to Hamilton. They struck up a brief acquaintance. And Christine, familiar with that city shared her ample knowledge of it.

She chose travel aboard the *"Free Trader"* because it would stop at Oakdale. All along their route thus far Christine had observed schooners and scows at docks unloading iron rails and wooden ties for the back-breaking work on the railway, Toronto to Montreal. As they left Kingston, an Irish girl questioned her about the Martello towers. She was pleased to be able to share information that she had learned about them. They docked briefly in Coburg and then viewed Port Hope while on Lake Ontario.

The busiest wharves were in Toronto. Many boats of various types were heading in to dock. A deck hand identified schooners, steamers, brigantines, and barges carrying lumber, stone and wheat. Their captain followed a barque, a three-masted ship into port. About twenty passengers disembarked. It took nearly half an hour to unload their luggage. *"Was it just over sixty years ago that Governor Simcoe had laid plans out for the city?"* Christine mused.

Outward bound they passed Port Credit and Christine's heart skipped a beat. *"We'll soon be in Oakdale Harbor. I wonder if Uncle Randolph received my timetable?"* They slowed to pull in safely to one of the wharves. Christine wished her traveling companion well. She clutched her reticule and carpetbag and grabbed the rail as they came to a bumpy stop. The gangway was lowered and she made her way carefully to the dock below.

"Christine, oh Christine. I'm over here, lassie." A familiar voice reached her ears. Uncle Randolph had driven himself, but had hired help to load her trunk and carpetbag. She curtseyed and shone her bonniest smile. He gallantly took her hand and kissed it. A wave of relief engulfed them both and they hugged briefly. *"Ye look so well, uncle,"* chatted Christine, *"and happy too, I see!" "And my what a*

fine young lady you are – and what adventures ye have had!" returned the pleasant man.

The staff at Bon Adventure heard the whinny of the carriage horse and rushed to present a line at the main entrance. Tears of joy overcame Christine and Mrs. McKay as they clasped hands. This time Christine accepted the maid's help. Janet burst out an *"Oooh!"* when she unpacked the luxurious wolf coat. Christine praised the kindness of the one who had given it to her.

Uncle Randolph wanted Christine to meet his intended bride. A small dinner party was set so that she might meet Sylvia Reid. Their first encounter went very well. Sylvia shared a love of animals and enjoyed doing handwork. She had often walked Randolph's Gordon setters for him on the estate. Christine observed that they listened intently to each other's opinions and liked to be close to one another.

Her first week back, Christine assisted her uncle in his office – taking dictation so that she might do some correspondence. Mid-week she translated two letters for him from French to English. She began to work in the garden – planting evening primrose and pansies. Toward the end of the week Randolph reported that he had invited a number of her old friends to dinner Saturday evening. Mrs. McKay was to plan the menu. Christine insisted that she help Janet set the dining-room table. She brought daffodils and forsythia from the garden to brighten the main rooms.

Mrs. McKay produced her famous chicken stew. It was accompanied by light scones made from freshly churned butter. Apple crisp, from dried apples was served as dessert. Christine welcomed Laura Ross and her suitor, Joseph, the minister and his wife and Joshua Van Allen. Christine, Laura, Sylvia and the minister's wife were left in the parlor while the four men retired to Randolph's study to smoke and enjoy a liqueur.

Christine knew that she had changed since her arrival from Scotland. Her adventures and travel with Duchess La Fleur had made her more confident, more mature and without her realization, more beautiful. Joshua seemed to be a shy young lad to her now. She noted awkwardness in his manner toward her.

It was a Friday afternoon in late April. Christine was working in the flower garden on the east side of the house. She looked fresh and delightful in a blue gingham day dress. The white pinafore apron that covered it was edged with eyelet. As she put on her uncle's old gloves she bent to plant violas, the color of highland heather. She stood up momentarily to stretch her limbs. From nowhere rushed a tall dark figure. He bumped her sending her flying into a soft leaf pile. It took a second for her to recover her breath.

Somewhat amused at first, Christine's blue eyes sparkled – but they became more serious when they confronted a set of deep brown eyes. The young man effortlessly helped her to her feet but his eyes never left hers. Time seemed to stop. They were transported to a plane of existence where they were the only ones. As she brushed off her dress and gathered the remaining plants and tools into a basket, she felt confused and flustered. He felt a deep tenderness toward her and yearned to cup her face in his hands and kiss her. But the moment passed.

Christine stood tall and composed – then asked, *"And who might ye be rushing about like this?" "Forgive my haste, lass. You seem unhurt. Might ye be Christine MacDonald?"* She nodded. *"I'm Graham Sutherland, yer Uncle Randolph's new assistant. I've just arrived from Toronto by stage. I was visiting an old friend of my family's and didn't have time to inform Mr. MacDonald of my exact arrival time. I thought I heard someone singing. Was it yerself?"* Again she nodded.

They followed a walk to the front door. A trunk, carpetbag and brief case were waiting at the entrance. The butler, Robert summoned Stuart, the houseboy to assist while Christine led Graham to the parlor. "*Would you like tea, Mr. Sutherland?*" she asked. He answered, "*Yes, please Miss MacDonald*" and Janet who was dusting in the room was sent to fetch a tray.

Chapter 15
Events of May 1855

Each spring ships from Britain brought thousands of immigrants to the Canadas. The cities and small towns located on the Great Lakes and rivers swelled in population. Graham, a new university graduate was anxious to meet Randolph MacDonald's requirements. He was sent to Toronto to do land searches and under Randolph's tutelage began to write up wills, mortgages and insurances according to the laws of the new land. Christine was most valuable to both the men as secretary and translator. She took dictation, wrote letters in an excellent hand, made deliveries to people, banks and other establishments, often accompanied by Graham.

On her return from her travels Uncle Randolph insisted, *"Now ye must know how to ride. A horse can take ye in the fresh air to see our beautiful countryside."* Christine, who had not had this opportunity, was excited. *"I'd be most pleased to try! I like your Arab, Whitelocks. She looks bright and not as high to mount as yer thoroughbred, Nighthawk."* At first she was so busy assisting her uncle that she had no time for lessons. But when Graham arrived

Randolph placed him in charge of riding sessions. They were to be held three times a week, late afternoons. Christine fashioned a pair of riding pants so that she could ride astride. At first she became acquainted with the mare – feeding her carrots and sugar lumps – then leading her on halter. The second week Graham insisted that she mount and walk, following him on Nighthawk. They advanced to a canter within the confines of the paddock. Then they explored the estate, not yet venturing on to the busy road.

One afternoon they were cantering along the beach, part of the estate. Graham was ahead on the thoroughbred when he brushed a low thick willow branch. It snapped back and hit Christine, knocking her off her mount. He quickly turned his horse, grabbed the rein of the Arab. He tethered them both, then quickly rushed to her side. She had landed in soft sand. His arms circled her as she was helped to her feet. His deep brown eyes met hers. Time stopped. He gently took her face in his hands and kissed her warm lips, as he recalled he had wanted to do the first time he had laid eyes on her. They were both surprised at their reaction to one another. But silence was in the beauty of the moment. Christine looked at her pants, began to brush herself off, and came out of her trance. Graham frowned and asked, *"Are ye sure yer all right?"* as he brought Whitelocks back to her. *"Oh, aye! Thank ye!"* she could now respond. But was she really? Her heart seemed to pound and her lips tingled. And why did she want to be back in his arms?

The evenings at Bon Adventure were comfortable times. The lawyers, young and old would sit across from each other at the parlor's hearth, drawing leisurely on their pipes as the fire dimmed. Christine would sit near an oil lamp reading or stitching. Discussions were of business, Scotland, world affairs, families and friends.

The three of them attended Kirk regularly. Here Christine introduced Graham to Laura and Joseph, her fiancé. The two men struck up an immediate friendship. Joseph owned a birchbark canoe and invited Graham to paddle the river of a Sunday afternoon. As the month became drier, they hiked up the Indian trails that followed the river north.

May was coming to an end. Malcolm MacDonald, Christine's Father and his housekeeper, Margaret Fraser, were due to arrive. The schooner, *"Albion"*, built in Oakdale in 1853 had taken a load of lumber to Quebec City and was returning up river and into Lake Ontario with passengers. It was a joyous reunion for the three MacDonalds. The reverend's manse was still under construction so Randolph opened his home to his brother in the interim. And with the lawyer's wedding imminent, it would be helpful to have Margaret assist Mrs. McKay. *"Would ye announce the banns at Kirk next Sunday?"* requested Randolph. *"And would ye do me the honor of standing as my best man?"* he continued. Of course, Malcolm agreed in both instances.

Christine's birthday arrived May thirtieth. *"Could it be possible I have been in Canada a whole year now?"* she mused. She was stepping out of the teens and would be twenty. So that plans could go forward secretly for a dinner party of friends, Graham was asked to take her to the afternoon launching of a newly constructed schooner, the *"Two Brothers"*. Mr. McDonnell, its owner, attended Kirk and had invited the congregation to the ceremony and an afternoon's sail aboard. At one o'clock, dockside was humming with townspeople, visitors and seamen. The ship was christened with champagne by the mayor. A great shout went up. Oakdalers constructed many lake boats and were proud of it. Youngsters rushed on board followed by anxious parents, then those with more patience crossed the gangway. Graham offered Christine his arm. Christine flushed and said, "*Thank ye, I'm sure,*" as she raised her long skirt slightly to overcome an obstacle.

Christine noticed new residences and docks in the Burlington Bay area. They passed Pentland Castle of the McNairs and Christine shared some of the events that had taken place there last fall. They turned around in Hamilton Harbor. The afternoon had passed pleasantly. Christine took Graham's arm more than it was offered. He didn't object, but smiled obligingly. The *Two Brothers* arrived in port at five thirty. The chaise and morgan had been kept by the inn's hostelry for the afternoon. The two young people walked arm in arm from the docks to pick up their transportation.

While they were away, Uncle Randolph had summoned Sylvia and Laura to assist the preparations for the party. Their fiancés would join them later at supper. The ladies helped set the birthday table with pastel candles and bouquets of daffodils and tulips from the gardens. Ribbons were stretched from the chandelier to the four corners of the dining room. A pork roast was to be served with all the trimmings, and a lemon soufflé, Christine's favorite dessert, was to culminate the meal. Uncle had also invited Reverend McClung and his wife. Clara was an accomplished pianist and agreed to provide a program appropriate for a birthday celebration.

Members of the party lined the front hall. Uncle Randolph and Christine's Father stood at the head of each line. As the butler opened the door to the returning couple, the group sang in chorus *"Surprise! Happy Twentieth Birthday, Christine!"* Her eyes sparkled and her cheeks pinked with pleasure. *"Thank ye, my kind friends and family. What a surprise!"* she confessed. The delicious meal was presented at six-thirty. Christine took time to change from her day dress to her elegant rose taffeta. The company split into two groups, the men drifted into the library and the ladies into the parlor.

Shortly after eight Clara sat at the piano and began to play Scottish airs. Her husband at that signal brought the men out to join the ladies. Their voices blended in *"O! Ye'll Take the High Road and I'll Take the Low Road."* When she began *"Annie Laurie"* Christine and Graham sang in duet. They earned a hearty applause.

After an hour's musicale, Christine was ushered to a place of honor, a high-backed lady's chair that was turned to face away from the fireplace. Gifts were presented one at a time. Her new friend, Sylvia had embroidered pillowcases and Clara gave her a hand stitched bureau cover. Laura, with a soft smile, helped her open her gift; a white cotton nightgown trimmed with lace and whispered, "*This is for your hope chest.*" Her Father gave her a soft green plate adorned with birds that had been her Mother's. Her uncle carried his gift to her in a wicker basket with lid. She heard muffled noises within. He opened it and out peeked a puppy, white with black spots. *"He's an English Setter, my dear,"* he explained. Christine's eyes widened as she cuddled and stroked it. "*What a dear wee soul. I'll have to name him well! O! Thank you.*"

Graham, waiting patiently for his turn, asked, *"And does this remind ye of a wee incident, lass?"* It was the statue of a white horse. She certainly did recall his first kiss and blushed to the delight of everyone. She composed herself and said with deep feeling,

"Thank ye all for being with me on my special day. I am most grateful to ye for the special gifts. I will treasure them indeed!"

Chapter 16
Prepare for Change

The month of June would bring surprises, some pleasing and others challenging. In the first week, Christine received a letter from Matthew. All was going well at Halifax Citadel, but he had an urgent request to return to Scotland to help his Father deal with the illness of both his Mother and sister. Post haste Christine responded, wishing him well. She also admitted that she was in love with her uncle's assistant. This she hoped would free Matthew to find another.

As this would be Sylvia's second marriage, she and Randolph chose to be married in a quiet ceremony, with few friends and family present. For the service and going away she wore a burgundy suit matched with a cream-colored blouse, embroidered beautifully. Christine fashioned her bouquet of soft, pink peonies combined with fragrant mock orange blossoms. Sylvia's chest of linens and china had been sent ahead to Bon Adventure following a Scottish custom. Mrs. McKay and Margaret Fraser teamed to produce a cold collation for the wedding luncheon following the service. The happy couple was booked on an early afternoon steamer traveling east along Lake Ontario. They would stop at points of interest and finalize their two week honeymoon in Montreal to enjoy its theatre, concerts and fine cuisine.

Christine named her new puppy, Beau. Graham coached her in his training. He was to learn to sit, stay, lie down and to walk to heel - enticed by a morsel of raw meat. The most important command was to come to call. Graham worked hard with her on this. He hoped that when Beau responded quickly he could flush out pheasant, partridge and grouse on a fall hunt.

Early the second week of her uncle's absence, Laura Ross made a hurried visit to Bon Adventure. John and Joan McRae's second child had been still born. Joan had not allowed time between pregnancies. *"I've offered to make the tiny shroud,"* she said. Graham was present and interjected, *"I'll make the coffin, tell them. Would your uncle mind if I use the workshop, Christine?"*

"I think not," she responded, *"and I'll ask Mrs. McKay and Margaret to bake for us. Perhaps Sarah McClung will offer their home for the meal following the service."*

At the McRae's small home the little coffin was set between two chairs. According to Scottish tradition two candles were lit and placed – one at its head and the second at the foot. The family sat vigil in the day, but at night two men of the kirk sat four nights before the burial. At the graveside Reverend McClung read the service. Earlier one of the men of the kirk, tolling a bell, led the procession to the site. Usually the pallbearers and the mourners were men. But on this occasion Joan insisted tearfully that she must be present as her little one was laid to rest and it was allowed.

Post service the evening meal was a solemn one. The reverend asked the blessing, and Sarah McClung, Mrs. McKay and Margaret served a hot meal of lamb stew, scones and bread pudding. Following a prayer for the comfort and strength of the young couple, the company embraced each of them and left quietly on their homeward way, many wiping tears from their eyes.

Christine and Laura renewed their afternoon visits. Christine finished working a sampler which read: "*Christine Anne MacDonald born 1835.*" With Laura's help she cut out a dress to be worn in her role as bridesmaid at the wedding of Susan Morton and Captain Whitson. Laura was an excellent seamstress. The two young ladies worked together on it and when it was completed and fitted Christine looked charming. The gown was of soft blue muslin. The high neck was trimmed with white Belgian lace and the three-quarter sleeves had a touch of the same. It had a blue silk lining and a hoop at the hem.

The gardens were Christine's favorite places to work. She would go out early morning before the dew had quite burnt off to weed and water. The vegetable garden was hidden behind a hedge, separating it from the flower garden, and could not be viewed from the house. Drawn as a bee to honey, Graham would catch her there. He'd plant a kiss on the back of her neck. She'd be startled, but then somehow end up in his arms seeking a more leisurely one.

The May apple blossoms had filled the air with their sweet odor and falling petals. Now the droves of bees were buzzing around the fragrant June roses, filling the estate hives with honey. One early evening Laura and Joseph visited. The two couples sat on wooden benches on the flagstone patio at the rear of the house. Christine sat near Graham. She looked cool and lovely in a summer gown, soft yellow green and tiered. And as she flicked a lacey fly swatter back and forth his heart seemed to swell in his chest for the love of her.

The honeymooners returned. Christine relinquished her set of special keys to Sylvia. She realized that her role as chatelaine had come to an end. She and her Father were just visitors now. Would Sylvia assume her office duties as well?

In Port Credit, Reverend MacDonald's residence was close to completion. Malcolm noticed his daughter was uncomfortable when his brother and new wife returned home. He invited Christine for an early morning walk in the flower garden.

"Would ye like to join Margaret and me in the manse? We'll be just a few miles from your Uncle Randolph and Graham by boat or by chaise." Christine was at this moment so happy to have her Father here in Canada. She did not hesitate, *"I'll help ye unpack and settle in, Father. Perhaps I can help Margaret sew new curtains for yer new house!"*

After supper that day she had an opportunity to tell Graham of the new plans.

She thought that he would be upset that she was leaving.

"Ye know I'll miss ye, my darlin'." As he held her hands he explained, *"But I'm wanting to show ye how much I love ye – and it's not allowed 'til we are joined in marriage. Perhaps a bit of separation is best for us both at this time."*

Chapter 17
July 1855

On July second Reverend MacDonald and Christine received a visitor, an adherent of the Kirk in Port Credit. He happily announced that the manse was within days of completion. Could they be ready to occupy it Friday next?

Margaret was sent ahead with kitchen utensils and bedding, also perennials and vegetables already half-grown to start a late garden. Quality bedsteads and mattresses would be bought in Oakdale and transported with them.

Christine's Father had just unpacked necessities on his arrival. A trunk containing books, winter clothing and household items had been stored in Randolph's attic. Her own trunks (one of which stored her treasured wolf coat), were brought down from the same location and were quickly filled to capacity. A chaise and cart, both with drivers were provided by her Uncle. Graham had been given a lengthy assignment in Toronto and was not home to wish them "*Good-bye*" or "*God's Blessing*."

Their new home was equidistant from the Kirk and the harbor. The builders had preserved two large maples in the front yard and three mature spruce as a border at the back of the property.

Bearing their carpetbags they climbed quickly down from the chaise. The Scotsman assigned to greet them rushed to assist their driver and houseboy with their four trunks and bedsteads.

They followed a rough stone path toward a pleasant residence. Its walls were of sandstone quarried locally. Its portico held seven pillars. The main door was between the second and third one, with the seventh providing a small open porch for the kitchen, set back on the right. There were four large rectangular windows, two on either side of the main entrance. The dormer jutting centrally on the roof would surely provide a bedroom. Christine dropped the large brass knocker. The sound echoed through the house, but no one came. Her Father opened the door. They entered a small foyer. But as they suspected a staircase led directly to the dormer room above. Suddenly the back door flew open. In rushed Margaret, hands and apron dirtied from her time in the garden. "*Welcome to yer new home!*" she greeted warmly. "*I was just tending to the vegetable garden when I heard ye arrive. I'll just set the kettle on for tea. Ye must need some refreshment after yer trip.*"

It was quickly determined that Christine would have the dormer room as her bedroom. Her bedstead, trunks and carpetbag were borne up by the three assistants. Margaret's bedroom was off the kitchen and just back of the dining room. Her Father's was behind the parlor. As a minister must have a study, a small corner of the large parlor was screened off.

Christine breathed deeply of the refreshing pine odor found in the new house. Her attention had been focused on the immediate. Suddenly she had an empty feeling. Graham, her love was far away.

When bedsteads were assembled and mattresses in place, Christine and Margaret worked as a team to make them up with fresh linens. All three members of the household retired early, exhausted by the requirements of the move.

Saturday morning Christine spent digging and planting the lettuce and tomato plants donated from the gardens of Bon

Adventure. As they sat at supper that evening a knock interrupted them. Christine answered the door. She found Graham, carpetbag and briefcase in hand on the porch. *"I took the last stage from Toronto and decided to stop off to see how my lassie was getting on,"* he explained, enjoying her delight. She clasped his free hand and led him into the dining room. With excitement in her voice she asked, *"Would ye have extra on the stove to offer this young traveler, Margaret?"* The housekeeper was happy to prepare a plate for she quite liked this young man. Reverend MacDonald realized that Graham had taken the last stage. He offered, *"Surely ye'll need a place for the night. Would our couch in the parlor do?"* Graham agreed, delighted to have more time with Christine. Margaret busied herself in the kitchen. The Reverend excused himself and returned to his study, preparing for his first sermon at the Kirk the following Sunday morning. Graham had arranged to return to Oakdale late that afternoon.

The young couple had the evening pretty much to themselves. Christine took him to the wharves at the mouth of the Credit River. When they returned she took him on a tour of the house. More than once they had an opportunity to embrace and kiss. They were thrilled to be in each other's presence.

"I shall search through all the lands, in the valley and on the mountain, in the church and in the market, where is he whose hand and eye are gentle"[1]

The Morton Whitson wedding was to take place the following Saturday. Christine obtained her Father's permission to go, accompanied by Margaret as chaperone and assistant. Margaret arranged that a Scottish neighbor would provide MacDonald with lunch and supper daily while they were away. They would return by the following Tuesday.

Susan looked radiant in the off-white lace wedding gown that she borrowed from Elizabeth. Christine helped to create the bouquets. The bride's was of dark red roses. The two attendants carried nosegays of white daisies. Ann and Victoria dressed in white muslin gowns tied with blue sashes carried baskets of rose petals. William bore a velvet cushion that held the gold wedding bands. Christine, beautiful in the soft blue muslin and

---

[1]Welsh (16th century) translated by K.H. JACKSON from the book "*Celtic Verse*" – edited by Elaine Gill and David Everett – England – MacKays of Chatham 1998.

Susan's friend, Clara, also in blue completed the wedding party.

The service was conducted by the army chaplain in the chapel at Fort Henry. Captain Whitson's troop formed a guard of honor as they left the church. The young girls had a wonderful time scattering fragrant rose petals before the happy couple. The Whitsons then left on a short honeymoon to Montreal by steamboat. They were to reside in the married quarters in the barracks on their return.

Christine amused the three children and directed their reading and writing assignments during her short stay with the Walkers. Yet she was anxious to return home. She had promised Margaret that she would help her make the drapes for the windows of their new home. Also she needed to catch up work in the law office at Bon Adventure for she had been absent for more than two weeks.

When she returned to the manse her Father gave her a letter. It had been re-directed by her Uncle. The correspondence, written in French was in the Duchess's hand.

"My Dear Christine,

I trust that you and your family are well.

I have been very busy since my return to England. During the past three and a half months I have renewed many old friendships. The two symphony concerts I attended were marvelous! I also took the opportunity to see the Shakespearean play "The Taming of the Shrew" with friends.

I have sent you a box containing daffodil and tulip bulbs. The daffodils are English. The tulip bulbs I obtained when I visited The Lowlands last month.

I am planning a trip to France in September. I have been invited to visit two cousins, one in Calais and the other in Paris.

Your June letter told me of your affection for Graham, and his for you. I pray your relationship will flourish and grow.

I hope to hear of your recent activities.

With Love ~ Janine (Duchess La Fleur)."

Chapter 18
August, 1855

Days were sunny and warm. The rains fell adequately, mostly at night when people slept. Gardens were bursting with squash, pumpkins, beans, tomatoes and other vegetables. The fruit trees bearing peaches, pears, plums and apples filled the air with a mixed fragrance. The farm crops of corn, wheat, oats and barley were bountiful. Wagonloads of winter wheat were reaching Oakdale Port. Arriving from the north and west the grain would be shipped to wheat hungry England.

In Port Credit Christine, Reverend MacDonald and Margaret were getting settled in. The ladies worked daily, making lined burgundy damask drapes for the living room and dining room windows. Margaret was learning where she could obtain fresh eggs and milk, meat and fish and other foods. Reverend MacDonald was visiting a new member of his congregation every other day and was often invited to stay for lunch. Christine was continuing to add to her hope chest: pillow slips embroidered in cross stitch, and a tablecloth with eight napkins.

After a four-day stay at Bon Adventure Christine was caught up with her office backlog. Three letters required translation. She sat with Graham at Kirk Sunday and they were invited to lunch at Laura's. It was then that Laura and Joseph asked Christine and Graham to be their attendants at their wedding early in September. As it was her second marriage, Laura said that she would wear a brown velvet gown with a jacket. After some discussion it was agreed that Christine would wear a teal blue dress of a similar design.

Graham drove Christine home in her Uncle's chaise and stayed for dinner. He left early to travel back before dark because of possible danger. It was reported that a hungry bear had attacked a horse last month on the same road.

Christine felt an immediate void and concern. The emptiness persisted most of the week. Each night she hugged her feather pillow, imagining him in her arms. But this provided little solace. Her full joy would be realized Thursday when she would see him again at Bon Adventure.

Graham was experiencing difficulty of a different kind. A red-headed gal at Kirk determined that he would be fair game now that Christine resided in Port Credit. She fluttered around him like a moth drawn to a light whenever she encountered him. She seemed to know when he visited the bank or the barber. She would appear suddenly like the Huntress Diana poised to conquer. He would graciously bow and say politely, "*Good day, Miss Bridget,*" and step back several paces to avoid her nearness. He would envision Christine's lovely face at moments like this. His feelings of annoyance and anger would deflate and a peace would come over him. Each of these meetings cemented his conviction that Christine was his only love.

Graham purchased a bay mare and a gig early the next week. So when Christine finished her two-day assignment Friday night he proudly drove her home. His plan was to stay overnight and on Saturday to help her Father build a small tool shed.

Saturday while the men were at work, Margaret and Christine washed, then sliced early apples and strung them to dry for the winter. In the afternoon they cut many cabbages to make a barrel of sauerkraut to be used only in the cold months when fresh greens were not available. The odors of apples, vinegar and fresh cut wood mingled in the clear air. When everyone had freshened up for supper, they enjoyed homemade vegetable soup, cold ham and fresh bread.

Graham suggested an evening walk to the harbor. Walking arm in arm the couple found a small park near the calm lake. They sat on a rough wooden bench. As they held hands, a scene of magnificent beauty unfolded before them. The sun was setting; it was producing a panorama of gold, turquoise and pink. A half moon began to rise and rippled in reflection on the lake's surface.

Without hesitation Graham began, "*Ye know how much I love ye, Christine. And ... I know ye love me too.*" He reached inside his vest pocket and brought out a small box. "*Will ye marry me ... be my wife?*"

"*Oh, yea, I love ye dearly,*" she blurted out, tears beginning in her eyes. They sparkled in the dimming light. Graham withdrew a lovely ring – a band of alternating sapphires and diamonds which caught the moon's light. He gently took her left hand and placed it on the fourth finger.

"My Mother gave me this ring and had me promise to present it to my one and only love." He lifted her hand and kissed it. *"And now it is done!"* He took her face in both hands and kissed her – at first tenderly, then passionately.

They realized that they were being observed by a strolling couple, so reluctantly moved apart. Graham spoke quietly, *"We can't expect my parents to attend our wedding, dear. I've received recent news from my Father. There is a smallpox epidemic in Scotland, and as doctors are scarce and often falling ill themselves, he is needed."* They talked on, agreeing that they would marry in early October.

It was dark when they reached the cottage. Graham kissed her goodnight at the entrance. She headed straight upstairs, admiring her ring as she went. Graham located Reverend MacDonald in his study. They sat opposite each other in the parlor. *"I have come to love yer daughter, Reverend MacDonald"* began Graham comfortably. *"I have asked her to become my wife and she has agreed, sir."*

"Ye know Christine is not of age 'til next May, Graham. But I have observed how kindly and devoted ye are to one another. How could I

not give ye both my blessing?" responded her Father.

Reverend MacDonald committed to reading the banns of marriage at his new Kirk. Because the young couple knew more folks in Oakdale, they would request Reverend McClung to perform the service there. They also hoped that Randolph and Sylvia would agree to hold the wedding reception and dance at Bon Adventure. Sunday morning Margaret and the Reverend noticed and admired Christine's ring and warmly congratulated them both. The Réiteach, the informal engagement party would take place mid-September at the manse.

While Christine was at Bon Adventure the following Thursday and Friday, many plans were made. Randolph was very pleased to hear of their engagement. He presented them a remarkable gift. *"My dears, please accept our gift of four acres of land from the estate for a new home. We will sever it soon, Graham. I understand that you have a legacy which will come due when you marry. You have said that it will be sufficient to build a sturdy home. As to the wedding party and dance, Sylvia and I agree – it must take place here where the space is adequate."*

Christine and Graham expressed their gratitude to the MacDonalds. They were pleased that arrangements were proceeding smoothly. It would be convenient to reside close to the legal office. Graham was working hard and was hoping that he would be worthy to be Randolph MacDonald's law partner in the future. Christine persuaded Graham that she was passionate about establishing a school that would offer French classes.

Through his legal contacts, Graham learned that a railroad entrepreneur was going to England midsummer, returning in June of the following year. He was seeking occupants to rent his home in town for that period. Graham swiftly put his name forward. Rental properties were scarce in the young community.

Chapter 19
September, 1855

Swallows and grackles were gathering in large flocks to migrate south. The night air was sharp, but the days were sunny and warm, even though daylight was shortening.

McKlintock, the tailor, carried a few readymade suit-dresses. Christine was able to purchase the ensemble in the size and teal color that she required. Joshua Van Allen had heard of her engagement at Kirk and came forward shyly to congratulate her.

Laura and Joseph Stewart were married on the first Saturday of the month. The service and small reception were held in the minister's home. Laura had not traveled on the water for some time so she requested that they journey to Niagara Falls by steamboat for their honeymoon. They were looking forward to their stay at the luxurious Clifton House.

The week that they were away a frightening incident caused concern in town. Early Thursday morning the people were awakened by the deafening clanging of the bell of the Church of England. Six firemen rushed to their station, harnessed their anxious team to the water-wagon, dressed in oilskins and hats and sped to the harbor. A grain elevator was burning furiously sending smoke and ash into the morning sky. The townspeople had already set up a bucket brigade at its base. Internal combustion was the culprit. The firefighters propped a ladder against a safe side and two brave fellows mounted it, shouldering a large heavy hose. By the time they had extinguished the blaze there was but a charred skeleton of a building remaining – all that the honeymooners would view on the waterfront as they returned home by boat.

In spite of the excitement, legal work continued at Bon Adventure. At the Friday noon break, Sylvia knocked on the office door and opened it slightly. "*Could you come upstairs for a moment, Christine? I have something to show you.*" Sylvia pushed the bedroom door open and let Christine enter. There arranged on the bed was an exquisite white lace wedding gown. "*I was wed in this dress many years ago, my dear. It is so beautiful that I could not part with it. I used to be your size, but alas, no longer. Is it to your taste?*"

Christine was mesmerized by its delicacy. It looked hand crocheted, yet it was not heavy as she lifted it. It had a soft white silk lining. She fumbled for words, then blurted out, *"Oh it's a beauty! I haven't much time to look for a gown. Are ye certain ye won't mind?"*

"Not at all, Christine. Then that's settled! You will look just lovely in it!" added Sylvia happily.

The same afternoon Christine finished her office work before three and requested from her Uncle a mode of transport to town. She realized that she needed to acquire linens and blankets for the bedrooms of her new home. She ordered three sets of cotton sheets at the General Store. Then Stuart drove them north on the river road.

They soon arrived at the woolen mill, its heavy machinery audible as they approached. Its sheep, grazing contentedly were in a fenced field east of the factory. For the comfort of the workers, the large entrance door was wide open to let the air blow through. Christine left her driver, Stuart, to water the horse and she entered the dark interior. The wool, cut in June, had been washed then stored on the main floor. An apprentice was feeding large amounts into the wool picker where it was loosened.

"This wool will be sent upstairs to be carded then spun into yarn and wound on spindles. The spindles will then be returned to the lower floor where the fibre will be tied on the loom in an organized pattern. Then the weaving will begin," explained a plump lady just inside the door. She was knotting the ends of a grey blanket as she spoke. Immediately the foreman came downstairs carrying an armful of spindles. Christine waited 'til his arms were free.

"I would like to order two white blankets, sir. Would they be ready by the end of next week?" she asked.

"Certainly, Miss," he responded. He strode to a high desk in the corner. *"One moment please while I record your order in the ledger. They will cost three dollars and fifty cents each when you collect them."*

When they returned to the estate Graham was ready to take her home. The mare was keen to go, but Christine asked him to wait a few more minutes. She went to the kitchen where her pup Beau was sleeping in a wicker basket. She gently touched his head telling him, *"Be good, now for Graham."* He was still learning to come to call so it was best to leave him in training at Bon Adventure for now.

The engagement party for Christine and Graham was held in the Port Credit manse three weeks before the wedding. On the Saturday evening many friends from Oakdale joined there: Uncle Randolph and Aunt Sylvia, Laura and Joseph Stewart, Reverend McClung and his wife, Sarah, John and Joan McRae, Christine's Father, Malcolm MacDonald and Margaret Fraser. Graham according to tradition arrived at the house alone.

"May I have a Bible, sir?" he asked of Christine's Father. The requested object was to be representative of the family's vocation. A new family Bible was given to Graham. Then he asked for Christine's hand in marriage, received a hearty *"yes"* from her Father, and hearty applause from the approving company. The evening gathering continued with songs of their homeland and dancing to music provided by a fiddler and a piper both volunteers from the Kirk. The delightful event closed with good wishes and a hearty toast in whiskey to the feted couple.

A week before their wedding they set out their gifts to be viewed in their rented home. Graham's parents sent a set of dishes, white china with gold trim for special occasions. Wealthy cousins of Christine shipped a set of cutlery in silver – stored in a rich walnut case. Christine prized her Father's gifts, an Austrian crystal fruit bowl and hand-painted milk pitcher. These had come down from her Mother's family. Margaret Fraser had made her a cotton peignoir. The Duchess's gifts of spring bulbs and a silver tea service were interesting to most viewers. Joan McRae had embroidered two tea towels from bleached flour sacks; these were highly treasured for Christine knew that they were hardly affordable. Laura and Joseph's gift was linen towels for their washstands.

One Thursday evening they were at the house. Graham pronounced, "*Christine, dear, I know how much ye have wanted to teach. Would ye like the use of the study for a few students? Ye could begin late October. I think I can do all the work I need at the estate. I have heard of four families that want small classes and French lessons for their children.*" Christine was deeply touched by his kind offer and amazed by the information he had collected.

"*Oh, Graham, yer such a dear!*" she exclaimed and rushed over to give him a hug.

Chapter 20
October, 1855 – The Scottish Wedding

The first Saturday of October was the designated wedding day.

Margaret Fraser teamed up with Mrs. McKay to bake the rich fruitcake and to plan for the reception. They had fun wrapping and hiding buttons and several sixpence in the cake for unsuspecting guests. The mansion was to be sparkling clean so they hired Joan McRae to assist them.

Christine and her Father joined the household mid-week to help direct the preparations. Her chest or kist was now filled to capacity with mostly handmade items. It was sent ahead to the cottage unlocked and unbound. Graham accepted the Stewarts' invitation to stay with them three nights before the service.

On the advice of Uncle Randolph, the couple had invited the businessmen of Oakdale and their wives. Thus Graham would continue to renew his contacts.

The anticipated day arrived. The sunny morning was a good omen. *"Happy the bride the sun shines on."*

Christine rose early and with Stuart, the houseboy's help, picked flowers from the garden for the wedding bouquets and the reception tables. She fashioned her flowers in a circle – its center of clustered pink roses surrounded by small white mums. Out of it trailed three pieces of English ivy and a ribbon of the tartan MacDonald. The second arrangement to be carried by Laura, her attendant, became a nosegay of white mums. Margaret helped her to place sweet peas and mauve and white mums in vases to decorate the buffet table in the dining room.

Then Christine began to prepare herself. She bathed and washed her fair hair, pinned small curls to the top of her head and allowed the rest to fall softly about her happy face. Margaret brought her a light lunch and sat beside her. *"I wish my Mother and brother could be part of this day,"* she spoke softly, a distant look creeping into her eyes.

About two o'clock, Sylvia knocked at the door. She looked fashionable in an olive green suit dress, its jacket trimmed with corded piping. *"May I help ye dress, dearie?"* she petitioned.

As Christine stood in her petticoat in the middle of the room, Sylvia lowered the exquisite gown over her head. It slid down and fitted perfectly. The elbow length Juliet sleeves were not lined and so showed the lace to advantage. The v-shaped neckline allowed her to wear a single strand of her Mother's pearls. The skirt flowed gently from a narrow waist to the floor. And after she stepped into her new, white, leather pumps she declared, *"Aye, I'm really quite comfortable."*

"Ach, ye are a vision," murmured Sylvia. And at the same time she thought, *"She could be the daughter I never had."* At this she gave her a quick hug.

Christine gazed at her reflection in the floor length mirror. She was satisfied. Lastly she attached a coronet of roses to her topknot.

As she reached for her bouquet, she heard the approach of Graham's gig. He had sent Joseph and Edward, his friend from the bank, as *sens.* They were to convey his bride, Christine, to the Kirk as it was done in Scotland. The rest of the family was to follow. Uncle

Randolph had rented a landau, a much larger vehicle for the occasion.

The town clock struck a quarter to three. Laura and Joan McRae made sure that Graham was ready. Christine had arranged this escort. They walked on either side of him to the Kirk. He remembered the Sutherland motto, "*Sans Peur*" (*Without Fear*) and walked along resolutely. He was handsome, indeed. His trousers were of the dark ancient Sutherland tartan, green and black striped by red and white. His jacket was a rich, dark green velvet. Not being partial to ruffles, he chose a simple white shirt.

At three o'clock Reverend McClung walked calmly down the nave of the Kirk, the congregation rose and he stood, Bible open, in front of the altar. Graham and Joseph followed him, side by side and stopped at the right. As Edward and Joan silently joined their spouses, all heads turned toward the main doors. The organist began a Scottish march.

A young, bright bride, arm in arm with her Father began to process. She smiled warmly and nodded to several of the assemblage as they made their way to the altar. Matching her step, Laura, her matron-of-honor followed. Graham was fascinated by Christine's every move and marveled at how beautiful she looked. As her Father released her he whispered that he agreed to the union. As he sat down in a pew nearby, Laura was given the bridal bouquet.

The service began. The minister's rich voice flowed with Psalm 91: *"He that dwelleth in the secret place of the most High shall abide under the shadow of the Almighty."*

The questions of commitment were asked. *"Do you, Graham, Robert Sutherland take Christine, Margaret MacDonald as your wedded wife?"* A warm resounding *"I do!"* rang throughout the sanctuary, and Christine's response was just as sure. The groom then took the gold band from the best man and handed it to the Minister. As he held it, he spoke of it being an object without end. He then returned it to Graham and he asked the groom to place it on Christine's fourth finger. As Graham held her left hand, the Reverend declared, *"I now pronounce you man and wife."* A second psalm, the 95th was read clearly and resolutely: *"O come let us sing unto the Lord: let us make a joyful noise unto the rock of our salvation."* A short, but sincere prayer followed. The

Reverend asked that rich blessings be poured upon the newlyweds and all present. Then Reverend McClung took them aside to a small table where they signed their marriage certificate.

Joyous music broke forth and the newlyweds, arm in arm progressed to the double doors which had already been flung open. They stood together, hand in hand on the Kirk steps, greeting family and friends. As they headed for Graham's gig, many folk threw rice or petals on them. When they got seated, they in turn, threw coins into the reveling crowd.

A long cortege of horses with conveyances bearing joyous people followed them to the estate. Graham lifted Christine down like a piece of fragile china. Robert, the butler, greeted them with congratulations. They stood at the parlor door to greet everyone. They were grateful to be joined in the receiving line by her Father, Randolph and Sylvia.

The tartans of the MacDonalds, Sutherlands and Stewarts were given special recognition that day. The ladies were in their best for the occasion: their gowns provided a symphony of colors and textures created by velvets, silks and taffetas in rich fall shades.

Photographs were taken of the couple in the garden. The bank manager, McIsaac and his wife, had hired a photographer for them as a wedding gift.

When the guests had seated themselves around the parlor, the pair returned. They were offered a dram of whiskey, which they drank from the same glass. "*To the happy couple*" a guest voiced and all the glasses went up and the amber liquid down. An anonymous voice began the "*Marriage Wish*" joined by all the Scots present. *"May you have a long, happy life, a sound and healthy body, a cottage which does not leak, and a meal chest which is always full."*

At the butler's announcement that the buffet was ready, Graham and Christine led the party to a lengthy table laden with baked salmon and roast chicken, and green beans, squash, peas and mashed potatoes as the vegetables. As the large number of guests sat about at small tables set in both dining room and parlor, the butler and maid presented them a tray of various pies to choose from for dessert. At last, Robert wheeled in the large wedding cake on a trolley. It had already been cut into small pieces so that Christine and

Graham could go about and serve it to their guests.

The spacious parlor was cleared to provide a dance floor. The celebrated couple encouraged the company to join them in a schottische. Soon many pairs formed in circles for this round dance. The piper, violinist and pianist blended together and separately to supply music for the evening. When the crowd tired, the pianist rendered songs of Scotland and they participated heartily. And before the evening ended, according to Highland tradition, Graham as the groom carried a basket about in order to receive a monetary gift from all who attended.

The festivities came to an end about eleven o'clock. Stuart and an assistant had prepared torches for each conveyance. It was a grand sight as the company drove around the fountain, down the lane and toward town.

As Graham and Christine arrived at the cottage Reverend McClung and Sarah caught up with them. The torchlight from outside helped Graham to locate and light two oil lamps. Graham's Mother could not be present so Sarah agreed to act for her. She broke a piece of shortbread over Christine's head. Then she prayed that Christine would be a good wife. They thanked the Reverend for the blessed service and bade their friends, "*Goodnight.*"

Chapter 21
The Honeymoon – Toronto 1855

Suddenly they were alone. For a while they sat on the sofa, wrapped around each other, exhausted by the day. It had been one of preparations, people and promises. Their young faces, reflecting in the firelight of the hearth, spoke of hope and love: their eyes often came together in deep tenderness.

At last Graham rose, reached for her hand and together they slowly climbed the staircase. As they opened the door to the master bedroom Christine could see the coverlet turned down and her new nightgown draped there. Sarah had arranged them for her. Graham discreetly left and changed in the neighboring bedroom. The pitcher on the washstand held warm water. She sprinkled lavender into the basin. As the water joined it the soothing fragrance began to drift out into the room. Graham returned and extinguished the two large candles on the dresser. Then they turned to each other for the deep love and compassion that their bodies and souls had craved to express for months.

After a light breakfast, they spent some time exploring the house. They walked about in the garden, commenting on the fall flowers, and picked three squash they found growing there. A bench was in a sunny location so they sat and discussed their visit to Toronto. They planned to see Fort York, a play and to attend a concert.

A maid came with the house. Flora was on holiday this week, staying with a cousin in Hamilton. But this attentive, hard-working Irish girl had left them a cold lunch: a meat pie and apple crisp.

They began to pack their trunk together, but the fires of passion lit again. When the mantel clock rang half-past four, they realized that it was time to dress for supper. Graham had reserved a table for two at the Royal Exchange Hotel.

After a quick breakfast Monday morning, they heard a whistle. Jake had arrived by trap to take them to the new train station. The Grand Trunk Railway had begun service to Toronto that year. Graham bought two-return tickets at the wicket. Christine wondered how she would manage the noise of the engine and the smoke of its stack. But all was forgotten as she quite enjoyed travelling, clickety-clack along the track at forty miles per hour. The rich fall colors of red, gold and rust filled the landscape mile after mile.

The engineer began to apply the brakes well before the small brick station. When the stop was complete, the conductor placed a stool on the platform at the base of the exit door. As Christine was assisted down she felt excited. This was her first extensive visit to the city. On her arrival from Scotland she had been whisked through on a stagecoach. And, when she had returned to Oakdale from Montreal, she had just come into harbor but had not disembarked.

The Mansion House on Yonge Street was to be their residence for the week. A gig was hired to get them there. They were shown their spacious room and they settled in. They were on the second floor facing the street. The extensive balcony outside their door would provide a place to sit in the evening.

After a delicious lunch, they determined to walk down the city's main street. Graham had a purpose for visiting The Bank of Upper Canada. They approached a solid, red brick building fronted by four white columns. Graham opened the huge wooden door for Christine. He led her to a comfortable black couch and walked confidently to a wicket marked: *Information.*

"May I see the manager, please? Would you present him my business card?" he requested of the young clerk.

"Certainly, sir, I'll be back in a moment," obliged the youth. After a short time the fellow returned. *"Please follow me, sir. Mr. Oliver will see you now."* Graham was directed to an open door along a short passageway. *"Mr. Oliver, Mr. Sutherland,"* the clerk announced quickly, then he disappeared. *"How may I be of service?"* questioned the manager.

"I am a lawyer working with Mr. Randolph MacDonald of Oakdale. I have been asked to introduce our firm to you by my employer. Should you or any of your depositors require legal services in our town, we would appreciate your recommendation."

"Our city, indeed the towns of our province are growing rapidly, I'm sure that you will be successful, Mr. Sutherland. Please leave me a number of your business cards. I will be happy to support an honest firm. My best wishes to Mr. MacDonald." Graham was very pleased with this meeting.

As it was late in the afternoon, they returned to the hotel to prepare for supper. That evening Graham and Christine were partners in a rubber of Bridge. It was here in the games room that they met the Williams. This young couple was visiting the city from Dundas. The four promised to meet for dinner the next night.

After a hot breakfast on Tuesday, Graham and Christine joined many pedestrians window-shopping. After some time they found themselves at Front Street, following the promenade and enjoying the view of the lake still alive with many boats. They watched craftsmen constructing a schooner. They observed boats being unloaded at various docks. Their products were taken by cart or wagon to the dockside warehouses. Goods from the United States and abroad had to reach land before freeze-up. Walking east toward Yonge Street they could see the sails of the Gooderham windmill, rotating smoothly in a south-west wind. Turning north on Yonge they spotted a sign showing a teacup. They entered this pleasant tearoom for lunch.

On their way back to their residence, they paused at the Cawthra Drugstore.

Christine purchased a sack of lavender and a fragrant bar of lavender soap. They reached the hotel, freshened up and joined the Williams in the dining room for supper. After a short walk the two couples settled down in the lounge for an informative conversation. They learned that John Williams owned a masonry firm. He claimed that he was very highly sought after in the Hamilton and Dundas region.

Early Wednesday morning Sutherland and Williams strode south to set up appointments with an excellent photographer for later that day. They returned mid-morning and Graham and Christine strolled to the shop of Joseph Rogers, a prominent hatter and furrier. His shingle above the door bore the picture of a top hat. The mannequin in the window wore a raccoon fur coat. A bell jingled as they entered the shop and it alerted a clerk who was hand-sewing a fur muff at the rear of the store. *"I am looking for a gentleman's beaver hat and for my wife a warm winter bonnet,"* Graham requested of the young man. A clerk, more senior appeared through the back door.

"Simon, I'll take care of this young couple," he declared and the younger chap returned to his workbench. *"Mr. Rogers has a*

superior collection to offer you," continued the confident man. And so Graham and Christine came away with just what they requested and more. They added a man's fur hat and a muff to their purchase.

It was time for lunch. They turned in to a restaurant serving "a catch of the day". Their next stop was at the portrait studio of Richard Coates. They arrived in good time for their half-past two appointment. He posed them turned toward each other and seated on a burgundy velvet settee. What a handsome couple his camera had captured! He immediately asked their permission to display a copy of their portrait in his main window.

After their approval Coates directed them to the St. Lawrence Market. *"Proceed south on Yonge and walk east on Front Street to Market Lane,"* he advised. They passed the odorous fish market as quickly as they could and were pulled north toward the hum of many voices and the frequent shouts of marketers offering their wares. Coates had also warned, *"Watch your purses in the busy crowd, won't you?"* Graham found a beautifully tooled leather belt at one of the stalls. Christine sought Belgian lace to trim a pair of pillowcases. A neat middle-aged matron produced a selection for her – adding that her sister in Brussels was her supplier.

The Sutherlands had arranged to meet the Williams at the White Swan Hotel, located at the north-west corner of the market for six o'clock supper. Together they enjoyed roast partridge with seasonal vegetables and shared a large bottle of French wine. They spoke of their experiences of the day and praised the excellence of Richard Coates' work. Dusk was approaching and the activities at the farmers' wharf were waning. They walked east along Front Street, but before the bridge over the Don River, hailed an empty cab. The ladies, wearing fragile shoes and heavy petticoats and carrying packages, were tiring. They were most pleased with their young men who had thoughtfully provided a twenty-minute rest on their way back to the Mansion House Hotel.

The shops were open at nine o'clock. The Sutherlands had an early breakfast Thursday. They had passed a shoemaker's several times and now looked for his boot-shaped sign. It was Graham's first winter in Upper Canada. He chose a high black leather boot which had probably been manufactured in the United States. Christine selected a beige lace-up leather boot with a low heel.

They hired a hansom cab – a vehicle for two. Its sides were closed and the driver sat above and behind them. They rode south, then west on Front to University Avenue. As they continued north, Will, their driver, drew their attention to the prestigious Osgoode Hall on the east side. Much later they were shown York General Hospital, founded in 1829 and King's College University established in 1827. They turned east on Queen Street to Church to view Knox Presbyterian Church, a building erected just two years before. "*Would you pick us up Sunday at fifteen minutes past ten so we may attend service?*" Graham asked their guide. Before returning them to their hotel for lunch, Will insisted that they see the Post Office on Adelaide at Jarvis and the remarkable home, *The Grange*, residence of Sir William Campbell.

The afternoon was sunny but the air sharp as they marched south to the newspaper office of "*The Albion*". Graham placed an advertisement in it for the law firm. It read: "*Messrs. Randolph MacDonald and Graham Sutherland, Barristers at Law practise in Oakdale, Ontario. We can expedite all your legal requirements. Our new office opens November 25, 1855 on Lakeshore Road."*

After taking afternoon tea, they returned the long distance to the Mansion House Hotel to meet their friends, the Williams, for supper. Near dusk the four young people set out for an evening walk. The Yonge Street sidewalks were of cement now and along their route lamplighters were beginning their task of lighting the gaslights. Special constables were walking about. These were men, citizens of the city, assigned to keep the peace at night.

Friday morning the Sutherlands purposed to walk north from their residence. After four blocks they began to encounter an acrid odor; it was that of a tannery. They decided to turn back. An early lunch was in order for Will and his hansom cab would be returning to take them sightseeing. At two o'clock the cab arrived. Graham assisted his love aboard and they were off on another adventure.

Fort York had been rebuilt after its destruction in the War of 1812 with the United States. The buildings: blockhouses and barracks were manned by British troops. They observed sentries on guard. Most of the cannons were mounted pointing south toward Lake Ontario. They were not welcome to enter the compound. As Will turned the cab east along Front, he pointed out the location of the Old Ford. Further along they noted a Georgian Front and were told it was the Custom House. At the foot of Yonge, Will pointed out the past location of Freeland's Soap and Candle Factory.

Earlier in the week the hotel manager had obtained theatre tickets for the two couples. Friday's fish dinner enjoyed, the young gentlemen assisted their lovely ladies into a waiting landau. They were off to Frank's Hotel on Market Lane north of the St. Lawrence Market. *"Ali Baba and the Forty Thieves"* had thrilled many audiences. The costumes of Arabian design, fashioned of silks, damasks and velvets fascinated the crowd and especially pleased the ladies. The men concentrated on the flash of the scimitars. The cave of the thieves looked authentic for it had been formed of papier mâché and then appropriately painted. Benjamin's landau bore them through a Fairyland, created by the glow of gas-lamps. The four spent the remainder of the evening in the lounge, conversing comfortably and sipping chilled white wine.

Saturday was the Sutherland's last chance to shop in the city. Christine's Uncle Randolph and his wife Sylvia had done so much to make their wedding special. They walked south to Monro's Dry-goods Store to look for a gift for them. They agreed on a small wall tapestry as their "thank you". It depicted a mid-summer English garden scene of thatched cottage and roses. Graham wanted to look into a tack shop at the sign of a horseshoe. He looked for some time at all of the items on display. To Christine's surprise he ordered a dark-chocolate brown English saddle. Was he planning to buy another horse when their house and stable were built in the spring?

The four friends had lunch together at the hotel. Earlier John had hired a landau. It took the young couples to Christie Spit, at the east end of the harbor. What an exciting afternoon they spent at the horse races. Of five races, Graham and John came up with two winners each. They both came away with more than they had wagered and were quite satisfied. The ladies, parasols up for the sun, enjoyed it all – but were taking close note of the fashions of the day.

The two couples returned to the hotel late afternoon. After a short rest, they met for a late supper. Part of the evening was spent, sitting on their upper balcony and watching activities in the street below. A stagecoach, filled to capacity with passengers and loaded with their luggage, thundered north. Farm wagons or carts drawn by a horse or two labored along bearing winter supplies to locations outside the city. Were they returning home from the St. Lawrence Market or carrying supplies from the dock warehouses to the merchants of many small villages and towns? They did not know. As the night air chilled, the fireside in the lounge beckoned. When they had settled in, they all ordered hot cocoa. As they realized that this was their last evening together, they exchanged addresses and promised to keep in touch with each other.

After a late breakfast Sunday, the Sutherlands, dressed in their best, met Will as planned. The cab carried them to Knox Presbyterian Church for the eleven o'clock service. The learned minister preached a sermon on the importance of prayer. He gave many examples of those who had received answers to their petitions in miraculous ways. As they paused for a moment on the front steps, a voice called out, "*Graham, young man!*" It was Graham's friend, Dr. Menzies who he had visited last spring and who had attended their wedding. "*By all means join us for lunch,*" invited his wife. "*Have your driver follow us home,*" ordered Menzies. It was all settled so quickly.

They arrived at a fine two-storey house on Jarvis Street. Graham paid the driver and asked him to return again at two o'clock. The maid took their cloaks. They followed the family directly into the dining room where a cold lunch was already set out. The topic of conversation was their week in Toronto.

Just before the clock struck two, Graham and Christine realized simultaneously that they needed to return to the hotel and pack. They excused themselves and thanked their hosts warmly as they quickly boarded the hansom cab that was waiting out front. Their packing done, Will returned for them at a quarter past three. The hotel bill was paid and the couple boarded the cab, reluctantly waving good-bye to their new friends, the Williams.

Their train pulled in to Oakdale Station at five o'clock. Uncle Randolph, visiting in town, remembered the hour of their return and kindly sent his chaise and driver to collect them. They had arrived home in record time. Flora had a hot meal ready for them and served them in the candle-lit dining room at seven. Over duck and dumplings they discussed their week. *"I know we didn't attend a concert, dear, but I hope you don't mind. I know that an orchestra and singer are to perform in the town hall next week. Will I get tickets for us?"* offered Graham. *"That would be wonderful, Graham,"* Christine agreed, *"for I think we will find this week too quiet after our time in Toronto."* They reviewed the highlights of their trip: seeing Fort York, the Gooderham Windmill, the horse races and the play *"Ali Baba"*. The ultimate event though, was the meeting of kindred spirits, the Williams, John and Martha. The honeymoon had been filled with love, happiness and memories which they would cherish.

Epilogue

In the waning months of 1855 household routines were established with the help of Flora. Graham assisted Randolph in setting up their new office on the main street of Oakdale. Christine began a private school at home. Six pupils attended to study reading, writing, spelling, mathematics and to speak French. The young Sutherlands spent evening hours with a Scottish builder, pouring over plans for their new house.

Mid-December Sylvia became very ill and took to her bed. She had a serious chest condition. Christine closed the school early so that she could care for her. One evening as she sat in her patient's room, reading by gaslight, a sudden flood of thoughts filled her mind:

"Here I am in good health. I've had many exciting adventures and have met many interesting people. I have the love of a fine young man. We are planning our permanent home. I have started my own small school. My Father and Uncle are living here. How fortunate I am!" She heaved a sigh of gratitude and satisfaction, not surprised that warm tears were filling her eyes.

Under Christine's excellent care Sylvia grew well. She was still unable to travel at Christmas, so the family celebrated at Bon Adventure.

By the end of April Christine had ten pupils. She moved the group to a large room at the rear of the law office. Their spacious house was ready for occupancy at the end of May. It would take time to furnish it for several pieces of exquisitely carved furniture would be sent from Graham's family residence overseas.

It was early July. The Sutherlands had invited Laura and Joseph to visit. They sat on the back verandah to enjoy the cool breeze from the lake. As they sipped glasses of white wine, they began reflective conversation.

"I do miss family, friends and some customs of back home," began Joseph.

"I sometimes long to see some of Scotland's historical buildings, castles and churches and of course her landscape of hills and lochs," added Graham.

"I miss the smell of the heather but not the sheep," Laura interjected.

Christine turned the conversation in another direction. *"Think of it,"* she said, *"Father could emigrate easily – and a position awaited him. I have not seen as much child labor here as in Scotland. The factories are much smaller here, too. Mr. Ryerson of whom we read is the Superintendent of Education for Upper Canada. He is working to provide education for all children."*

"You know, the tax system in Britain is punitive because of many wars. Here a tenant farmer can come to own land. He's given responsibilities such as road-making near his property, but pays no taxes," continued Joseph.

"In Scotland, unless you are Presbyterian you are not readily accepted," complained Laura. *"But here in Upper Canada Methodists, Baptists and other denominations are recognized, too. And now the Clergy Reserves of the Church of England are being sold to provide funds for public education."*

Graham would not be left out. *"It is good to know that King's College has a class graduating in law this year. Christine and I saw Osgoode Hall, a court of justice last October. Dr. Menzies has told me that medical doctors are being instructed at Trinity Medical College and Toronto School of Medicine."*

The Sutherlands were among the many newcomers to Upper Canada who were dedicating their energy and intelligence to promote its growth. Their motivation and methods would be of the utmost importance for the positive developments of the present and of the future.

Christine had entered into the enthusiasm of this new land. It whispered "*hope*" and shouted "*progress*". She felt that she was riding a wave that rose higher and higher. She hoped that when she looked down from her lofty crest that she would recognize situations – familiar and dear: a kind word, a deep faith, a helpful deed and a spirit of co-operation and justice. She was not to be disappointed.

Bibliography

Personal Information

Mrs. Simcoe's Diary

Lady Dufferin – My Canadian Journal
– 1872-1878

A Gentlewoman in Upper Canada – Journals of
Anne Langton 1830-1842

History

Upper Canada: The Formative Years,
1784-1841 – Gerald Craig

Toronto of Old – Henry Scadding

Dundurn Castle – Edward Smith

Niagara – A History of the Falls – Pierre Berton

Upper Canada Village – Christine Daumont

Culture

The People of New France – Allan Greer

Krieghoff – J. Russell Harper

Highland Clearances – John Prebble

Scottish Customs from the Cradle to the Grave
– Margaret Bennett

About the Author

Pat graduated from McMaster University in Hamilton with a Bachelor of Arts Degree and pursued a career as an elementary school teacher.

She was a member of Etobicoke Writers' Group when her first book, *Hillsburgh's Heyday* was published by Boston Mills Press.

For several years she has been part of the Earth Harvest Writer's Group in Meaford Ontario and has attended recent workshops.

Her interest in history began as early as five years of age at her Grandpa's knee. He had attempted to homestead in Saskatchewan about 1900 and shared many of his colorful experiences. Her fascination continued when she lived in Fort Qu'Appelle. The Grade 5 teacher took the class on a walking tour of the historical town which had a connection to the Riel Rebellion.

She hopes to provide the reader a short social glimpse of the rapidly growing region from Niagara Falls to Montreal in the 1850's and to inspire further historical exploration.

To contact the author: benkor@lynx.org